A FIELD WITHIN

T.C. SOLOMON

HOUSOLO LLC

Front book cover designed by MiblArt

Back book cover designed by Dragan Bilic

ISBN 979-8-9864146-0-7 (paperback)

ISBN 979-8-9864146-1-4 (ebook)

Published by Housolo LLC

www.tcsolomon.com

For my father, the living embodiment of second chances

"Out beyond ideas of wrongdoing and rightdoing there is a field. I'll meet you there."
-Rumi

Prologue

New town, new job, new start, and I'm already falling behind, Kevin thought as he coaxed Mr. Johnson's dislocated arm back into place.

"Argh!"

Kevin felt the satisfying clunk.

For both the patient and the doctor, the relief was immediate.

Mr. Johnson heaved. "Thank you."

"Glad we could spare you the sedation." Kevin smiled. "X-ray tech is on his way then we'll get you a sling and you'll be good to go. Please remember to follow-up with your primary doctor this week. It was nice to meet you."

A young nurse intercepted Kevin on his way to the doc box. "Nice one, Dr. Bishop. I haven't seen that technique before."

"Thanks ..."

"Becca." She pointed at her badge.

"Right, sorry." He flushed. "I promise to get it right the third time."

She laughed. "It's your first day here and there are six of us. All good, I get it."

"Thanks for understanding." Kevin sighed. "I'll circle back to you with the discharge paperwork."

Back at his workstation, Kevin stared at the computer screen, scanning his list of patients. *Crap, did I put that order in for bed 7?* "Diltiazem ... now where do I find you?"

"Just like riding a bike, right?" A baritone voice boomed out.

"Huh? Oh yeah, hey Ron. Right. Just like a bicycle," Kevin said. *Except the bicycle had two loose wheels and had caught on fire.*

The lanky, bald, medical director reached over and pointed at the screen.

"There it is." Kevin clicked the order. *He has an impressively thick mustache from this angle.*

"Don't forget to ask for help. We're all here for you. It only gets easier from here."

Kevin nodded. "Thanks again for everything, Ron. It's been great catching up with you."

"You bet."

Kevin quickly returned to the screen, tapping the tabletop.

"We're meerkats here at Chicago Legacy Hospital."

Kevin's nervous tapping stopped. "Meerkats?"

"You know, the mongooses. They're community animals. They keep an eye out for one another."

"Oh." Kevin nodded slowly. "Gotcha. That's nice everyone feels supported."

Ron pulled up a chair next to him. "Do you have time for a quick story?"

He didn't. "Sure." Kevin leaned back. *Don't forget to call the surgeon for bed five.*

"Back in med school there was a student in my class that was getting teased a lot. He was overweight, and kept to himself, so he was an easy target. But what people didn't know is he had just endured a horrible family tragedy. He was dealt a shit hand, but he ground his way to the top of our class at graduation, never sinking to the level of the bullies along the way. Look at him now." Ron pointed to the familiar textbook above Kevin, *The Pillars of Emergency Medicine, by Gregory Bishop, M.D.* "After all of your father's success, the happiest I saw him was the night he met your mom."

Kevin's hands slid up to the armrests. For the first time on the shift, he felt comfortable.

"I bring up this story for two reasons," Ron said. "The people I respect most in this life are the resilient ones. Greg didn't get into specifics with me regarding what happened to you at your previous job, but frankly, I don't care about the specifics. It sounded rough, and I'm sorry you went through it. I know you'll step up and fit in here because I know where you come from and what you're made of. Second, don't lose sight of who or what makes you happiest in life. That's what makes any of this worthwhile." Ron extended his hand.

Kevin shook it. "Thank you, Ron. I have a good feeling about this place."

"We think it's a good fit." Ron exited.

"Dr. Bishop, the x-ray's done." A recognizable voice called out.

"I'll take a look. Thanks Becca," Kevin said.

His hip vibrated. An incoming call lit up his phone. *That number ... is from Dad's ER.*

Kevin went cold.

His father knew it was his first day on the job, and he would never call unless it was an emergency. *Oh fuck. Fuck. What's happening?*

"Hello?"

"Kevin, it's Dad ... are you sitting down?"

1. ROOTS

Kevin pounded up the hill, headphones blaring. He hoped the screaming in his ears, and the racing of his heart, would drown out the sludge in his head, but his beloved Rage Against the Machine seemed too loud. His pulse was way too fast. *This is forty.*

Collapsing by the old tree, he searched for the carving in the bark. *There it is.* He touched his mother's initials gently. It had been twenty years since their last Sunday walk there; twenty years since her ashes dusted the roots of the lofty, solitary oak. *I wish you were here with me. I'm so lost. I'm numb. Please help me wake up.*

Kevin's gaze followed the trunk out to the leaves, just as they began to rustle. The gentle summer breeze reached his arm, curled around his shoulder and across the nape of his neck, filling him with a calming warmth. All five senses came into alignment. His mind quieted.

Kevin had forgotten what serenity felt like.

He took a step back with a knowing smile before descending the hill. Jogging in silence, his breathing settled into the cadence of his strides.

No more running.

Kevin closed the door behind him. The early morning light crept across the living room carpet. It was all familiar: recliner, corduroy couch, clunky TV, but home felt foreign.

He wandered to the dining room, or, more accurately, the study: one end of the dining table had been his desk when he was a teenager. His seat faced a large window, which meant it was also the portal to his daydreams. He tried to conjure a reverie now, but his newfound inner stillness was leaving him, and he was overtaken by something much darker.

Three shadows were sitting at the table. They each spoke in turn.

"Kevin, you made a series of clinical errors and you put a patient's life at risk. We cannot allow that to happen again."

"We have to do what's in the best interest of our community and the future of our group."

"This is your last day here."

Kevin had never responded.

The medical directors' silhouettes faded away. Then, there was another presence in the room, at the liquor cabinet to his right.

Mom.

"Don't tell your father," she whispered playfully, pouring a glass of whiskey.

Kevin glared at the throng of new bottles. *Dad, how can you still drink like this after what it did to Mom?*

He was startled by footsteps upstairs.

Pull yourself together. He slid from the doorway and crossed the foyer to the kitchen. He prepped a mug of Earl Grey: fifty-five seconds in the microwave. Start.

After placing a packet of Splenda on the counter, a framed photo beside the microwave caught his eye: his father giving him his first white coat in medical school. He reached into the cabinet for the animal crackers and slowly chewed a handful. *Are you still proud of me?*

"I didn't even hear you come in last night." His father's voice rumbled down the creaking stairwell. He emerged before him, a mountain of a man. More snow on the peak. *Damn it, how is he even bigger?*

"Hey, Dad."

Kevin hugged him and rested his head for a moment on Greg's shoulder.

"Thanks for the wet hug."

Kevin felt his dad fight his urge to recoil from the hug, so he pulled back. His father checked his own newly washed scrubs for imperfections. The microwave beeped. Kevin nodded at it and dropped onto a chair.

"How was your flight?" Greg asked. "Save any lives?"

"Uneventful, thankfully. Is Alex awake?"

"Yes, finally. He had a late night with friends." Greg pulled out the mug and added sweetener. "Perfect. Thanks," he said after taking a sip, then glanced at Kevin's book on the kitchen table. "What're you reading?"

"*The Subtle Art of Not Giving a Fuck.* Kind of like a self-help book. It's—"

"Other people's ideas of how you should live." Greg rolled his eyes and grabbed his white coat from its hook. He checked his pocket watch. "Action and experiences are what you need for real growth. Like what you just went through."

He just paraphrased a chapter.

"Thanks, Dad, I'll try to remember that."

Greg rummaged through his briefcase, found his badge, and transferred it to his white coat.

Kevin's eyes lowered.

"How are you?" his father asked.

If only it was a year ago, when he was a steady flame encased in glass. *I'm leaving LA and moving back in with you. How do you think I'm doing?*

"Living the dream."

"Look." Greg threw his coat over a chair. "They never should have fired you, but I warned you about that group. They run their new doctors into the ground, and you knew that when you signed the contract. You ignored the red flag."

Kevin gave him a defeated glance. "I couldn't focus."

"Of course, you couldn't. You were in no shape to handle anything else after your divorce. Kev, you were stretched so thin, but now you have time to heal. You'll make it through this. I've always been your dad, and your coach. I used to give you a kick in the ass whenever you got into a slump in baseball. This is no different."

Slump? I'm barely hanging on.

Greg leaned in. "Get out of your head. Trust your gut."

"I didn't tell you what they did." Kevin's voice cracked. "I reached out to Dr. Sunder to help me intubate my patient and he ruptured her trachea and blamed it on me. No one believed me! I'm so fucked up I went to Mom's tree today. God, I miss her."

His father's eyes reached out to him, as his jaw went tight. "I wish there was something I could've done."

"You did." Kevin picked at the spine of his book before meeting his father's gaze. "You got me in at Chicago Legacy, Dad. Thank you."

Greg nodded. "That was all you."

"I can't believe I start in two weeks."

"You'll be ready."

More footsteps. Kevin straightened.

Alex turned the corner and stopped.

"Hi." Kevin stood, matching his son's six feet.

Alex finished buttoning his shirt, said, "Hi," and grabbed his tie from where it was flung across his shoulder.

"I can help you ..." Kevin reached out.

Instead, Alex handed the tie to Greg, and they assumed their positions in front of the mirror.

"Morning ritual," Greg said.

Kevin sat.

"How's summer here in Chicago? Learning a lot from Grandpa?"

"It's Long Grove"—Alex focused on Greg's technique—"and yeah."

"All set." Greg patted his shoulders. "Jeez, those muscles. You're going to burst out of that shirt."

Alex blushed and adjusted his collar. He had a Hollywood face above a triangle torso with muscle definition that could grace the cover of an anatomy textbook. "Hardly. I haven't been in the water in weeks."

Kevin, predominantly a land mammal, always marveled at how he had produced a state swimming champion. "There's a YMCA down the street," Kevin said. "Lap pool."

Alex nodded. "I'll check it out."

"I'm really happy to see you," Kevin blurted.

Alex paused by the door before picking up his backpack. He turned to Greg. "I'll see you at the hospital. I want time to review that appendicitis case from our last shift."

Kevin reminded himself to keep breathing. *Slow it down.* "Have a good day at work. Your grandfather is lucky to have you as a volunteer."

"Thanks, Dad," Alex said.

Alex opened the door to the garage, but Greg stopped him. "I'm missing some of my cigarettes."

"Your cancer sticks? Sorry to hear that."

"I'm trying to cut back," Greg said. "Please don't."

"It's been a few weeks with no change, so I thought I'd help the process. How many times a day do you tell your patients to quit smoking?" Alex smiled and walked away.

"That kid." Greg's nostrils flared.

Déjà vu. You can't imagine how many times I've tried to get him to stop, Alex.

Kevin's medical knowledge came with a heavy price. He knew his father's vices were speeding up his doomsday clock, and that at the stroke of midnight there would likely be a brutal, sudden death.

Kevin couldn't afford to be visited by another shadow. "I think he likes having you around and wants to keep it that way."

Greg listened out for the sound of the car door shutting. "Speaking of, when are you going to tell him?"

"I don't know," Kevin said. "He's already disappointed in me."

"Sooner, the better. I think he'd appreciate any communication at this point."

You can't be serious, Kevin thought. *The tumor robbed Mom of her voice. What was your excuse, Dad, for not talking to me then?*

They had spent five months listening to the sound of bloody phlegm being suctioned from her tracheostomy, watching her marshal what little strength she had into her thumb to push a button that auto-fed her morphine into her fading veins. All the while his father had demanded round after round of radiation and chemotherapies, ignoring Kevin's protests.

Dad, I was trying to protect her living will and you shut me down. How could you not see that letting her go was the most loving thing you could have done?

Sometimes a prolonged death was just as devastating.

Greg opened the side door. "I want to show you something. Let's go out back," he said.

Kevin hesitated, then followed.

The backyard was a semicircular enclave surrounded by trees holding hands. The trees towered over their fallen comrades who had been converted into a fence. Young Kevin had added insult to injury by carving his initials into the planks in plain view of a dilapidated deck facing it. The trees now looked in mourning at a fresh pile of timber with a sledgehammer on top of it.

"Your summer project," Greg said.

Kevin balked. "Aren't I a little old for this? I can hardly assemble Ikea furniture, and you want me to build a new deck?"

Greg sized him up. "Seems like you're in good shape. Tear it down, follow the blueprint."

"What about the guys outside Callahan's? They need work and could get it done in a day. A one-man job will take weeks." Kevin glanced quickly at his father's swollen belly. *And it needs to be sturdy.*

"That's not the point. And you won't be alone."

Kevin watched his father head back inside. *Some welcome home this is.* He sighed and looked to the clouds.

A crow was circling above him. Little did he know the bird had found him too, and a splatter of shit landed in his eye.

Perfect.

2. Fill It Up

The Nightcap was a dive bar, but it was Kevin and James's dive bar. It was a place of dichotomies. A warm layover that often became a destination. Nostalgic, yet filled with people trying to forget. A horseshoe bar crowded next to a haggard pool table that smelled like stale beer with a flickering light overhead. It always flickered.

"Barkeep! Two more shots of the good stuff!" James's voice shook the small room. "Are you ready for this?" He chuckled and slapped Kevin's back.

Kevin struggled to mentally prepare himself, gulped it and grimaced. "Ughh, you always do tequila!" He made eye contact with the bartender, Luis, and discreetly tugged his ear.

Luis nodded.

"You know why I do it? Back in high school, that bad tequila night at my place? How many times did you puke, about fifteen?"

"Didn't I throw up right in front of your mom?" Kevin asked.

"Oh yeah! I told her you were on antibiotics and that you had 'one beer and it didn't sit with you right.'"

Their throaty laughter reached an old man at the end of the bar. He grumbled before returning to his thoughts in the bottom of his mug.

More shots came. Kevin pretended to wince. The water was a needed break.

"I had a feeling it was you guys." A raspy voice emanated from the office behind the bar.

"Judy!" They leapt from their stools. They hugged the bar owner, their valued friend.

"Let me see you." Judy leaned back slightly to peer through her obstructing salt and pepper bangs. Her rosy, round face glowed. "Wow, you both look great!" She ruffled Kevin's hair.

"But I look better than him, right Judy?" James puffed his massive chest out.

"After I messed up his hair, sure. But before, it's a toss-up." She ribbed James.

"This messy hair beats that buzz cut any day," Kevin said. James snorted.

"Now, boys." She jokingly held them apart. "Best behavior, please. We still have the table in the back if you guys want it."

"Always," James said.

The best part of *The Nightcap* was the back room. Behind a dirty velvet curtain was a round table with four chairs, a dartboard, and a frayed *2002 Women of the Beach* bikini calendar. A VIP room where they tried to make sense of their crazy worlds, and maybe laugh a little. There was an exit door always left ajar. No one entered without Judy's permission.

"I can't believe you're both back in town. How are you?" she asked.

"Good," James said and found his old seat closest to the curtain. "Well, Mom misses me and she's having trouble with her memory."

"That's really hard," Judy said.

"I'm just glad to come home and spend time with her."

"I bet she's happy you're back."

The hanging bell on the front door jingled. Judy squinted through a gap in the curtain at her new patron. "Hmm," she said, then returned to the conversation. "So, are you going to finally bring home a lady friend to meet Mom one of these days?"

James blushed. "Not yet. Still single."

Single.

Kevin's thoughts drifted to his father, alone in his crumbling castle for the last twenty years. The overgrown weeds in his backyard. His overgrown midsection. No dinner parties, no girlfriends. Kevin shuddered. *That can't be my future.* But was this year of bachelorhood much better? Filling empty nights with empty partners from dating apps?

"Right? ... Sticks!" James shouted.

Kevin shook away the image. "Huh?" Kevin was number eleven on their high school baseball team, and the number eleven apparently looked like two sticks. So did his legs.

"You still with us?" James laughed. "I don't see him for months and now he can't handle his liquor."

"Aww, go easy on him, James. He's gotta keep his mind sharp, saving all those lives." She smiled at Kevin and turned to leave. "Let's catch up more later. I'll have Luis bring you a pitcher. So glad to see you two." The drapes closed behind her with a small plume of dust.

"Speaking of saving lives, sorry to hear you left your job. That's rough," James said to Kevin. "You okay?"

"Thanks man. I'm hanging in. They forced me to do too many shifts. I was spent. Had to walk away."

James studied Kevin's face for a moment. He nodded and grabbed the pitcher from the bartender. "You went straight into one high pressure job after another. It's crazy you never took time off."

"Finally getting it now, I guess," Kevin muttered.

"Good." James took a few long gulps. "Peel away the bullshit. Like that crap with Susan. Long time comin'."

Kevin tried to shake the thought of his ex from his mind, push back memories of things he wished long forgotten. He still felt himself bristle remembering her unwarranted suspicions. "Did I ever tell you she didn't want me to grab drinks with my coworkers if women were there? She'd say stuff like, 'Don't you see enough of them at work? Why do you want to go so badly?'"

"Wow. When you're in the trenches with a team you need to blow off steam together. It's important."

"She didn't get it, and she didn't get me … One time, I told her about this perfect moment where I was body surfing with Alex in the ocean and I accidentally ended up in the barrel of a wave surrounded by walls of water. It had the coolest sound. Hypnotic. You know what her response was? 'I don't think you've ever done that.' Belittling me in front of Alex became a sport."

"Death by a thousand cuts," James said. "Did I just see Dr. Kevin Bishop get a little angry? Holy fuck, I never thought I'd live to see it!"

Kevin looked down at his drink.

"That right there." James pointed at him. "Stop that shit. You keep bottling it up, and one day you'll explode."

My anger isn't always under control. I just don't want you to see it.

"You were Susan's doormat. You kept her shoes clean. Not anymore."

"But I also worked on myself," Kevin said. "I went to therapy, and I told her we should go as a couple, but she wouldn't. Part of me thinks I quit too, and I could've kept fighting for us. Maybe I should have, for Alex's sake."

"Alex is a man now. He's in college. You left, and it was the right call. It's done." He reached out with his beer. "To new adventures."

Kevin met him with a solid cheers. "How's Coronado these days?"

"Really great." James's broad shoulders were tense.

Kevin shot him a puzzled look. "But ...?" He leaned in.

James slumped against his seat. "One of the new students is dragging the whole class down. He was lined up with his team, everyone working to carry a tree trunk over their heads, and his hands were barely on it. Poor kid in front of him tore his rotator cuff because of it."

"Seriously?"

"When I called the slug out, he blew me off. I mentioned it to the superiors, and they said I overreacted."

"What's up with this guy?"

"He's an entitled sack, nephew of the new commanding officer."

"I guess beating him into submission is off the table?" Kevin smiled.

"You need to stop watching those cartoons," James said.

"*Looney Tunes*? Never," Kevin said.

James shook his head and laughed. "But you may be onto something." He smirked and polished off his mug. His eyes softened. "Did I ever tell you about Brody?"

Kevin tried to steady his foggy head. "Was he the one in Afghanist—"

"Yeah," James said. "I keep in touch with his family. His sister Grace was Navy too. She lives here and she's a nurse now. You two should—"

Shouts erupted behind the curtain. Shattered glass.

"Stop it!" Judy yelled. "James!"

James was through the curtain before Kevin could stand.

Kevin entered to see the old man no longer at the end of the bar but sprawled on the floor. He was unconscious and bleeding. Kevin dropped to a knee, took out his phone light, and inspected a deep cut on his scalp. "Judy! Towels! Still have that glue?"

She nodded and disappeared into her office.

James kept Kevin and the old man behind him. He faced the attacker.

"Here come the Boy Scouts," the man growled, holding a broken beer bottle.

James slowly took off his jacket and laid it on the pool table.

The man's bloodshot eyes widened. "You military?"

James nodded.

"Army?" He gripped the bottle tighter.

"Navy."

A crooked smile appeared in his dirt-caked beard. "Just like me. Except I was doing tours when you were in diapers."

"Not like you." James rolled up the sleeves of his tight Henley.

Judy handed Kevin the supplies and retreated behind the bar. "He's a SEAL, you dumbass!" she shouted.

The man's face went white. The bottle shook.

James wagged a finger at Judy.

"But I bet we're similar in many ways. Tough childhood, right?" James turned his forearm under the light revealing a constellation of cigarette burns. "I've lived your anger. Anger at what was done to me."

The man's eyes darted around the room. He took a step back.

"And I know that pride. That push ... to show you're the alpha. Let it go."

Kevin's new patient moaned.

"He okay?" James asked, eyes fixed on his aggressor.

"He's good," Kevin said. "Closed a cut. That's it."

James raised both hands in front of him. "See? Everything's—"

The man bolted outside with the bottle.

Flood lights beamed through the windows. "Police! Drop the weapon!"

He fell for the stall tactic. Oldest trick in the book. There's literally a police station down the street. James picked up his jacket and put it back on.

The battered man wobbled onto a knee. "Bar," he mustered, as they hoisted him onto his stool. He held up his bloodied hands, confused. "What're we drinking?"

"This round's on me, boys." Judy snapped on a glove and grabbed the soiled towels. She cringed. "I don't know how you handle this nasty stuff Kevin but thank you."

"You're welcome," James interjected. "Anytime."

She squinted at him through her bangs. "And thank you for keeping it to one set of rags."

Test Subject 1
Interaction 2
Ford Hospital
010900SMAY19

Informed Consent for Pneuma Transplant

<u>Today we will be assessing whether you:</u>
[X] Understand the transplant process including the procedural details, risks, benefits, and alternatives
[] Express a choice on whether to proceed consistent with your preferences and values
[] Appreciate the consequences of participating or refusing
[] Show appropriate reasoning when comparing these consequences

[X]: Denotes the objective has been completed
[]: Denotes the objective is still pending

This interaction is being video recorded.

———

My interviewer Mr. Montoya enters, and gentle air fills the room, drawing me away from the paper taped to the table. *Is it Montoya? Montenegro? Something like that.* He strides over to the table and takes a seat across from me. Oh, he carries himself confidently.

I see my reflection in the large mirror behind him ... I look tired. *I should've touched up my roots. My memory these days.*

"Hello again, Ms. Trudy," Mr. what's-his-name says.

"Hello dear. Please call me Katherine."

"How have the accommodations been so far? How was your sleep?" he asks.

"Lovely." I twirl the cord of my nasal cannula. "Ya'll have made everything so comfortable."

"Of course, and please let us know if you ever run low on your oxygen. We'd be happy to supply you with another tank." He smiles.

That smile. That was Pete's smile! Oh, how I miss his face. The only man to ever show up in a suit to a first date. 'Clair de Lune' floats across my mind. I hope you're resting sweetheart.

I remember I'm being interviewed and slide my hands off the table. I don't want him to see my dusky fingertips.

"This session will be longer than yesterday. We would like to get to know you more."

"Of course." I search my arm. "I unfortunately don't have my patch with me. I would hate to be rude and leave for a smoke."

He looks puzzled. "You still smoke? I'm surprised to hear that."

"Yes." I blush. "Some things I can't let go."

"That's very interesting. May I?" He nods towards his briefcase.

"Of course."

He scans a document at an impressive speed. He nods. "I must've overlooked that."

"I used to hate that I smoked. I was disgusted with myself. Now, I've accepted that I enjoy it. I've made peace with it." He glances at my nasal cannula.

I laugh. "Even after the consequences I've felt. Don't worry, I turn off my oxygen when I do it."

"You seem happy. Why did you enroll in this transplant study?"

"Life ... This *gift* ... Is about quality, not quantity, and mine's been an amazing journey. I'm grateful for all of it, both before and after my trauma. It also affords me the opportunity to help someone and to be involved in something historic."

He nods thoughtfully. "We cannot thank you enough."

I smile.

"I'll get you a patch. Can I get you anything else? A water?"

"Oh no dear, you don't have to do all that! Very kind of you," I say.

"My pleasure, just a moment."

"What a process this has been. Thank goodness you're so much more personable than that stiff psychiatrist." *And so handsome.*

3. Recognition

"Time for me to go." Grace smiled. "Thank you for dinner. I'm blocking your number, so if you want a second date, you'll have to find me."

Kevin slowly finished his drink and placed the empty glass on the table. His eyes focused on the dimly lit wall of ancient celebrities. "I'm not big into games."

Grace tucked her hair behind her ear. "Me neither, but you have a lot on your plate right now. No rush." She stood.

"Are ..." Kevin awkwardly slid out from the table. "Are you sure you're interested?"

"See? All up in that head of yours. Oh, and you can't use James to find me. No cheating." She reached for her jacket.

Kevin intercepted and slid it over her shoulders. "Who are you?" he whispered.

Grace shrugged and walked away. She weaved through the tables, grinning back at him. Her eyes were stars under the lantern lights.

He slowed behind her.

She stopped at the door. "You okay?"

Kevin exhaled. "I don't know."

"Do you need to sit?"

He shook his head. "I'm good."

They reached the sidewalk. He took five more steps then winced, clutching the right side of his abdomen.

"Okay, what's going on? Seriously."

"I tried to write it off the last thirty minutes, but it's not going away."

"Do you still have your appendix?"

Kevin looked at her anxiously.

"I'm taking you to a hospital." Grace pointed through a park. "Chicago Legacy's around the corner."

"Please no, I start there next week."

She tapped her foot, focusing down the street. "Wait here." She grabbed her keys.

Ten minutes later they arrived at a different ER.

"Hi Ms. Lamoreaux." The hospital valet opened her door. "I thought you weren't working night shifts anymore."

Grace smiled nervously at the valet. "Hi Carl, not working. My friend's sick."

A tech arrived and helped Kevin into a wheelchair. He glanced at the young man's badge. *Saint Monica Hospital.* "Thanks Brian. I'm actually starting to feel better." Kevin slowed the wheels and smiled at Grace.

She squinted at him. "Better that fast, Dr. Bishop?"

"I feel like a new man."

Grace looked him over, probing. "Interesting." She came closer and reached for his abdomen to examine him.

He intercepted her hand softly and laced his fingers through hers.

"Or maybe"—her lips curled up at the corners—"you faked it all."

"I wouldn't say *all*. This, here"—Kevin held her hand warmly—"is something I can't fake, and I can't wait to see you again."

She blushed, unable to contain her full smile. Her hand returned to her side as she stood. "I'm glad you're feeling better."

"Time for me to go." Kevin pushed himself out of the chair and stepped back. "Thanks for a great night." He set off for the street.

She took a moment to regain her bearings, leaning on the armrest of the wheelchair. Her smile was still there.

Brian cleared his throat and gently jostled the chair. "Sorry I need to take this back."

"Oh, right … of course," she said.

"So … um, what kind of doctor is he?"

She looked up at the big blue letters of her hospital. "A sneaky one."

———

Three days later, Grace entered the parking lot to find Kevin resting on her bumper.

"How about that second date?" he asked.

She reddened and rocked back on her heels. "I have work I really need to finish."

"You sound like me." He reached for her hand and pulled her in.

The sunset streaked her porcelain cheeks. Her wavy brown hair smelled like a cascading rose garden, but it was her pheromones that captivated him, softening, and warming the air between them.

"Quick date, you pick," he said.

Grace arched back and gazed at the clouds. "You know what I've been craving?" She bit her lip.

The faux-frosted glass doors of Ice Dream opened, and Kevin was suddenly in a Disney movie. The aqua and white ensemble greeted their princess as two teenage girls gawked at Kevin, whispering to each other in their aprons.

"Who's that, Grace?" One giggled. "Boyfriend?"

"I'll tell you later." Grace winked.

Kevin picked a table on the sidewalk.

Grace took her first bite of Speculoos Fantasy smothered in marshmallow and graham cracker, then gave a contented wiggle. "I'm sure your job is pretty boring. No good stories or anything like that."

He chuckled. "I pretty much just stare at a wall all day. As an ICU nurse, I'm sure you've had your fair share."

She placed her spoon in her cup and leaned forward on the table. "Not like yours. My patients are mostly machines by the time they come to me."

Kevin saw his mom on her hospital bed gazing at him. He blinked it away. "What would you like to hear? Pick a category, please."

"How about crazy?"

"Crazy ... As in shocking, or crazy as in funny?"

"Both, but let's start with funny."

"Brace yourself." Kevin grinned. "In medical school during my first rotation, I had to do an abdominal exam on an obese patient. I lifted layers of his fat and found a half-eaten Twinkie."

"No!" Grace covered her mouth.

"Then the patient blushed and said, 'My wife and I play a game called *Find the Twinkie* and I think we might've lost that one.'"

Grace erupted with laughter. "Oh my God stop it. You're lying. No way did that happen!" She playfully slapped his arm.

"True story."

"That's priceless." She giggled through another scoop of melting ice cream.

He couldn't help but move closer.

"How about the shocking story? Do I even want to know?" she asked with feigned alarm.

Kevin took a moment. With strangers, he typically chose the French tourist who lost half his face after a bicycle crash at thirty mph. With James, it was the homeless man with a colony of squirming maggots that waved at him when he parted the patient's hair. For Grace, he chose something new. He wanted her to *see* him.

"It was my first pediatric death. She must've been seven years old." He fixated on the memory. "There was this horrible stillness while we waited for the ambulance. Doors opened, and the paramedics were performing these frantic chest compressions. She was in her swimsuit, wet on the gurney, and her arm brushed against me. She was so cold with this lifeless stare. Parents had left her with the babysitter and came home to find her face down in their pool. That image ... don't think I'll ever shake it."

She wrapped her arm around his and pulled him close. "I'm sorry you had to experience that."

He looked at her nestled against him. "Thank you. I don't normally tell anyone that story."

"What about your dad?" She sat up. "He's ER too, right?"

"Yeah, but he has his own set of tragedies. I try not to burden him." Kevin curled her hair behind her ear. "I'm glad you're here."

Their blue eyes met. "I think I'll finish my work another night. Let's get out of here," she said.

He followed her on Lake Shore Drive to her downtown apartment. It was Kevin's favorite road right alongside Lake Michigan. When he was at Northwestern for undergrad, he would play catch with James on the lakefill, and they would stop in amazement before turning home. It was their own private ocean.

"I don't think Jen's home." She gave him a flirtatious wink and opened her door.

"I do declare Grace, what're you implying?" he said in a passable southern drawl.

Grace dropped her keys on the table. "Want anything to drink?"

"Sure. Wine?" Kevin surveyed her large two-bedroom apartment. Clean, modern white fixings, flowers on the table, gorgeous view of the Chicago River. He saddled up to her breakfast bar and stopped on a framed photo. "King James at his coronation." He pointed. "Brody?"

"You've done your research." She handed him a glass. "Their graduation. We had James over for dinner that night and the rest is history. He had a standing invitation every month after. My Dad's a chef and never saw anyone who could eat like him."

"Bottomless pit."

"Brody admired him. So did I. James was the one who convinced me to do Navy ROTC in college."

"We should all hang out soon," Kevin said.

"Oh, indeed we should." Grace nodded as she slowly slipped onto his lap. "You and James are both only children. How did you not rip each other apart after all these years?"

"We've had our moments." Kevin leaned closer and kissed the top of her head, but then pulled himself back. "There's another only child. I have a—"

"Son?"

He froze.

"I've done my research too." She caressed his arm. "And I want a *man*. No more confused boys." She slowly kissed up the side of his neck and rocked forward, grazing his lips. "Know anyone?"

4. REBUILD

"You boys are tired." Kevin heard his father's voice above him, his head eclipsed the sun. "Taking a break already?"

They shared a look below Greg on the grass, sighed, and willed themselves to their feet.

Alex withdrew to recheck the blueprint on the backyard table. "I'm impressed Grandpa. You sketched these so quickly."

"Muscle memory. While you two had music and comic books, this was my 'quality time' with Dad."

. Alex wiped the burning sunscreen from his eye with his tank top. "What was he like?"

Greg checked their back posts. "His personality matched his job. Sharp lines and edges with expectations higher than his buildings. He acknowledged me on a good day and was a drunk reclusive asshole on a bad day."

"Sounds hard," Alex said.

"It wasn't all bad. My mother and sister were warmer, but even they were tough at times. You should've seen them when I walked away from the family business. They thought I was insane," Greg said.

"Medicine came calling." Alex beamed.

"It sure did, and it really is a calling." He turned to Kevin. "Does he know the story?"

"I don't think so," Kevin said.

"I was only a few years younger than you, Alex, walking on the busiest street in downtown Rockford. An old man in front of me lost his balance and fell backwards, breaking his back on a fire hydrant. I ran over and called for help because I didn't know what else to do. I thought he'd be screaming in pain, but as they were loading him onto a gurney, I could see that his legs were limp, but he didn't seem to feel anything. It was shocking, but I was compelled to find out how that happened. From that moment on, I had to know everything that made the human body tick."

Alex's eyes widened. "You found your blueprint." He glanced at his father. "Rockford ... Dad, wasn't that ..."

"Home of the Rockford Peaches." Kevin grabbed a hammer. "Remember, *A League of Their Own* when you were little?"

He did.

The movie had been on in the background; Alex had been more focused on his dad's smile after he hit a ball for the first time with his brand-new plastic baseball bat.

"Classic." Alex settled at his workbench and put on his goggles. "I'd like to go on a road trip there some—" He tried to pull back his words. *Shit.*

Kevin immediately saw it in his father's eyes. Greg was no longer with them in the backyard, he was on the side of the road, looking at the mangled, upside-down car. He could never turn away from the wreckage. Muted snowfall.

"There's nothing there anymore," Greg said.

Alex sank into the table and lowered his head. He grabbed the circular saw.

Kevin stiffened. "Be careful, use glov—"

The machine shrieked through the marked wood. Alex avoided his father's glare.

"He doesn't need gloves for that," Greg said, apparently shaking off the memory. "Glove will get caught under the guide rail then he'll lose a finger. You want me to go to work on my day off?"

Kevin saw Alex peer at him around Greg.

"Speaking of working." Kevin grabbed a handful of nails. "Dad, think you could help me with this?"

Greg put up his hands. "This is your project."

"I obviously have a lot to learn." Kevin squinted.

Greg hesitated. "I really shouldn't."

What? Okay ... Kevin turned and grabbed a plank.

Greg sighed. "I'll help with the side bands. It's an important step."

Alex crept forward. "Grandpa, are you—"

"I'm fine." Greg dismissed him.

They lowered the wood into position against the posts both on a knee across from each other.

Kevin paused. Greg's armpit sweat was rapidly spreading towards his middle. "Why don't you sit this one out?" Kevin asked. "Alex can help."

"Start hammering," Greg said through clenched teeth.

They pounded away, Kevin slowly rotating to keep an eye on his father.

Greg secured the last nail and squinted at the bubble in the level. His satisfaction was short-lived as apprehension took its place. He grunted to his feet and suddenly yelled in agony, grabbing his knee.

"You okay?" Kevin leapt to his side.

He flushed and lurched to the other post.

Alex wrung his hands. "Locked again?"

"Locked?" Kevin asked. "Did you tear your meniscus?"

"Think so," Greg muttered. "Few weeks ago."

Kevin put his hand on his back. "What do you need?"

"I'm fine. Just need to sit." He stumbled to the side door. "Go on without me. You've got it, Alex?"

Alex nodded. "See one, do one, teach one."

Greg smiled through the pain and then went inside.

Kevin tried to steady himself. "Why didn't you warn me?"

"He didn't want to worry you." Alex leaned against the table. "Why reach out when staying silent is so much easier, right, Dad?"

The words thudded against Kevin's chest. He lowered his eyes to the ground under Alex's scowl.

"Your relationship with Mom is none of my business. I get that, but you shut down on me too."

"Your mother and I care about you—"

"Dad, I'm nineteen! Stop talking to me like I'm a child. Be real with me!"

"You want real?" Kevin felt himself caught between the need to escape the shame of years of unatoned for mistakes and the need to defend himself to his son. He stepped toward him. "I love you. More than anything under the fucking sun and I failed you. You left for UCLA and then I left your mother. Pulled the rug right out from under you.

I had so much guilt, I couldn't look myself in the mirror. I still can't."

Alex closed his eyes. "The mirror? You haven't been able to look at *me* for a year." He opened his eyes and bored them into his father's. "I could've driven myself to Santa Barbara for that swim meet, but I asked you. I wanted time with *you,* but we sat in fucking silence for two hours! I pleaded for you to say something, and you said, 'Focus on what you need to do in the water today.' Really, Dad?"

"I didn't want to distract you with drama before your big—"

"Bullshit! Like swimming is more important than our lives together?! You stopped loving Mom. Did you stop loving me?"

Alex's words stunned Kevin. He was helpless to respond.

"How would I even know? You became so unpredictable, you were either a broken robot or raging against mom's 'control,' and you'd turn your anger on me. Do you know how many hours I hid behind my white noise machine? I was either missing you or afraid of you."

"I'm so sorry, Alex. That's why I couldn't look you in the eyes. I didn't know how to fix it. I ... I went to get help," Kevin said. "My therapist told me I was repressing everything, and then I started reverting back to people pleasing with your mom, which made me furious and—"

"It may have started with repression, Dad, but it became fucking neglect with me."

Neglect. The word gripped him. Clinically, he knew what it meant. He could see it written on the forlorn faces of his patients. But hearing it come from his own son squeezed out every remaining drop of self-assurance.

Kevin felt the urge to go to Alex's side; to shield himself from his own discomfort, but he didn't.

Not this time. Stay in this space. Sit with this.

"I'm so ashamed I hurt you like this. I was too absorbed in myself to see what I was doing to you. You know, I was your age when I married your mother. We were crazy about each other. I was so infatuated with her and all I wanted was for her to be happy. Then you came, and I wanted the same for you. I lost myself along the way, Alex, and I never felt like I was enough … I was always stuck somewhere between the past and the future, but never in the present. When I finally understood the damage I could be doing, I didn't have the courage to talk to you about it. That was unforgivable. But I did realize how much I needed to change, and I knew I needed a partner with more …"

"Warmth?" Alex asked.

Goosebumps rippled up his arm. "Yes. Someone who could take care of this." Kevin pointed to his own heart.

Alex nodded. "I love her, and I know she means well, but part of me is surprised you lasted that long." He rubbed his neck and slowly stood tall. "I can't believe you guys got married in college."

"Yes, we were young, but I don't regret a thing. I learned from it, and it gave me you."

Alex returned to the other side of the table. "Just don't shut me out again. I'll take this version of you over that zombie any day."

"Okay." Kevin stood by, encouraged. He watched as Alex picked up a wooden plank and sawed through the end. "Think you could help me with the next side band?"

Alex paused, sliding the goggles up his forehead. "Yeah."

They knelt, and hammered, nearly in sync.

"Speaking of women," Kevin said. "Any new ones in your life?"

Alex couldn't restrain a smile. "There's a nurse at work, Kate. She's older, of course, but she's so beautiful … Not sure if she even knows I exist. Not like it matters. I leave in a month anyway."

"A nurse." Kevin rocked back with a grin. "I'm sure she knows who you are. You're charming and easy on the eyes. You make an impression everywhere you go."

Alex shrugged and reached for the next nail.

"How are you feeling about medicine? Do you like the ER?" Kevin asked.

"I really do."

Kevin leaned forward to catch Alex's gaze. "I hope you know there's no pressure from us. I came to medicine later than you. I wanted to be a musician. It took me a while to agree with your grandpa and explore medicine, and even so, we had different reasons for becoming ER docs. He's always loved the science and being the man in charge. With me, it always came down to connecting with the person on the gurney and helping someone when they needed it the most."

Alex lowered the hammer. He looked at his father. "That all sounds great. I just hope I make it."

"You're smarter than us and you have the temperament for it, but that means nothing unless you have the will. My advice? Before you choose your path, figure out what fulfills you, determine the man you want to become."

Alex nodded. They stood up and stretched their legs.

Kevin glanced back at the house. "Be right back." He returned a minute later with a small carrying case. He handed it to him. "For you."

Alex gently rocked the gift in his hands. "Is this ..." His eyes widened. "No. You didn't!" He quickly unzipped the case and pulled out a beautiful mahogany ukulele. "Wow!" he said with full eyes. "Thank you." He threw his arms around Kevin.

Kevin squeezed him tight. *Music has always been there for me; I hope you feel the same comfort when I'm not around.*

"I can't wait to play it," Alex said. "You've got to get one too. It'll be like old times in the garage."

Kevin's hands slowly slid off his back. "Alex, I'm not coming back to LA."

"What?" He pulled back.

"They fired me at Charity Hospital. I need a new start."

"What?" His voice trailed off. "You're an amazing doctor. How could that happen?"

"I was burnt out. I made some mistakes and didn't document well. Then I was blamed for another bad outcome I had nothing to do with."

"Why didn't you tell me?"

"I'm sorry." Kevin stopped. Alex was placing the ukulele back in the case. "I didn't want to taint emergency medicine for you."

"Dad!" he pleaded, then shifted into defense. "There you go again. Ducking out." He slid the case back to Kevin. "This has nothing to do with you getting fired, but I don't want a pity gift. Go help Grandpa, I'm sure he needs you."

Kevin made his way into the kitchen, hands shaking. He had anticipated different reactions, and this was the one he feared the most. He had to lie down, but Greg was asleep on the couch and Kevin's air mattress was deflated. He somehow managed to carry himself upstairs to his old room. Few traces of Kevin remained: his bed with a chest at the foot and a bookshelf with a photo of him and James hoisting their high school district championship trophy. The room had become Alex's new dorm. His son's dirty clothes were clustered in the corner under a poster of Michael Phelps, his idol.

Kevin lay on the bed and stared at the ceiling. The quiet enveloped him, but he couldn't still his racing mind. Then, from below, he heard a note plucked softly from the ukulele.

Test Subject 2
Interaction 4
Ford Hospital
011300SMAY19

Informed Consent for Pneuma Transplant

Today we will be assessing whether you:
[X] Understand the transplant process including the procedural details, risks, benefits, and alternatives
[] Express a choice on whether to proceed consistent with your preferences and values
[] Appreciate the consequences of participating or refusing
[] Show appropriate reasoning when comparing these consequences

[X]: Denotes the objective has been completed
[]: Denotes the objective is still pending

This interaction is being video recorded.

———

If he keeps talking in that condescending tone, I'm going to carve out his tongue. Maybe I'll keep it on my keychain. My nails dig into the paper on the cold table. *What the fuck is wrong with me? Who thinks like that?*
    "Do you need more time?"

I hate his glasses and his perfect posture. "Do you need more testicles?"

"What does the photo mean to you?"

"Beach house. That's it."

"I need you to focus. What does it *mean* to you?"

The smell of Dad's spaghetti sauce. Mom dancing and laughing. "Where I met your mother. She was on her knees and—"

"Stop."

Hah! His pudding face is twisting. This is my room.

"What feelings—"

"This shit is pointless!"

He flinches. "May I remind you that you volunteered for this. Please be civil." He puts the photos away.

What a fucking farce. "Fuck civility. I can't do it!" I yell. "Isn't that the point of all this?"

Crawl into your hole little worm.

"Do you miss your family?"

There it is, pulling out his big gun. Compensating for his little dick. I try to crack his glasses with my stare. He fumbles his papers and adjusts his vest as he stands. So much nervous energy, like a gangly butler trying to save face after spilling a glass of wine.

He glances at the two-way mirror. "I'll be right back," he says, forcing a smile.

He reminds me of a cartoon I watched growing up. Dr. Bruce. So proper. Murdered by his lab rats. It was Halloween. The house smelled like—

The door slams shut. Muffled laughter echoes in the hallway.

You're … laughing at me? Now I'm your fucking amusement?!

My muscles tighten under boiling skin. *You'll be my Dr. Bruce. Come back. I have a gift for you.*

And it'll be hand-delivered.

My eyes stay low, away from the mirror, away from *them*. *Let's keep it a surprise.*

Minutes later, the door opens. I watch my target walk back to the table. I wait for the door to shut behind him.

Click.

I slam the table, snarling. "I heard you laughing. You pull that crap as soon as you step out, you fucking hypocrite? I will rip—"

"*Eeeeeee!!*" The overhead speaker pierces the room.

He cowers, backing away from my advance, mouth agape.

I'm going to ram my fist through it and out the back of his head.

"*Eeeeeee!!!*" Even louder. We can only clasp our ears. It chops me down to a knee.

By the time I refocus on him, he's exiting the room. I'm alone with the incessant ringing in my skull.

What's next, you bastards? I flick my middle finger at the two-way mirror. "I'm done. I want out. Do you hear me?!! End this right now!!"

Nothing happens. I leap to my feet and rifle the steel chair at the mirror. The dramatic impact leaves only a small crack. This infuriates me further.

The door slams open and guards rush in. I'm thrown to the ground in a coordinated attack. A knee presses on my back. I struggle for air as my wrists are wrenched behind me and handcuffed. They force me to my feet.

A suit enters the room. "Let him sit, please."

I'm flung into my seat. The guards hover like vultures.

"We did this for your protection, and, of course, we can't have you breaking things," the suit says.

"Fuck you."

High heels click and then stop behind him. "If leaving the study is what you choose to do, can we speak for a moment?" she asks.

My hands cramp underneath me. I can't focus. "I want these handcuffs off."

"We can take them off soon." The man nods and the guards transfer my cuffs in front of me and chain me to a bar on the table. "We just want to talk to you." He inches forward.

She turns to a guard. "Can you bring back a chair for me?"

I rotate my wrists trying to rub out the burn. They sit shoulder to shoulder, backs rigid. She looks familiar.

"I was told to give this to you." She attempts to hand me an envelope.

"Leave it on the table." I glare at her. "Are you aware of how to address me? You will *not* use the name I was born with."

They both nod.

"We've been behind the mirror since the beginning. We know," the suit says softly. High and tight sculpted hair, clean shaven. I bet this silver fox gets all the chicks at the nursing home.

She leans forward. "May we ask why you prefer that?"

"Who the hell are you?"

"Diane Dreucetti."

Then it hits home. *How many Asians have an Italian name like that?* It must be her. "Hello Senator." I grin. "I prefer to be called 'test subject,' because that's what I am."

"We cannot comprehend how frustrated you must feel," he says in a scripted voice. "We apologize for what happened with the last interviewer. He won't be returning. We promise to be more transparent. My name is Lawrence Kedge, and I work with Senator Dreucetti. We're both invested in this transplant study. During this process you've been asked a lot of questions. Now you can ask whatever you want."

I collapse back. "How many other people are you still interviewing?"

"Just one," Kedge says. "A good match for you."

I freeze on them suspiciously. *That means we're nearing the end of this.*

Senator Dreucetti smiles. "Do you still want to leave?"

5. A Day in the Life

Greg watched Jasper silence the cardiac monitor.

"Time of death, 18:25," Jasper said. "Thanks everyone. Strong work." He turned his procedural gloves into a slingshot and fired them into a waste bin.

Greg left the foot of the bed and joined Alex, who was glued to a wall in the hallway, nodding supportively at the exhausted faces of the departing nurses. "Good job in there, Oscar," he said.

"Thanks ... almost saved him." Oscar sighed, dabbing the sweat off his shaved head with the sleeve of his extra-large scrubs. He looked back into the room. "We'll get the next ..."

Greg quickly realized Alex was no longer listening to Oscar, he was watching Kate take off her mask.

Alex's knees buckled, then he pushed off the wall towards her. "You are ... uhh ... were amazing. I was watching you."

She cocked her head to the side.

"I mean I watched all of it, not just you." Alex flushed. "Just ... great."

Kate gave his arm a gentle squeeze and one last flash of her dimples as she passed. "Thanks Alex."

He loosened his tie and glanced at Greg sheepishly.

"Jesus." Greg walked back into the trauma bay.

Jasper, still next to the gurney, lifted an eyebrow at Greg. Greg nodded.

"Hey Casanova, come in here, I want to show you something," Jasper said.

Alex hesitantly entered.

"Remember to breathe," Jasper said.

"I've never been this close before," Alex said quietly of the lifeless body.

"Peggy, can you go check on bed six?" Greg waved the junior resident out and closed the curtain behind her. He lowered himself onto a stool in the corner.

"Crazy, isn't it?" Jasper shook his head. "Over time I can just tell the moment they're gone. Empty shell."

Alex glanced at the dilated pupils.

"We really appreciate your hard work this summer. You're doing a great job," Jasper said.

Alex smiled. "Thanks."

"But I'm sure you're tired of observing and stocking shelves. Want to get your hands a little dirty?"

"Yeah!" Alex exclaimed, reddening, as Greg gave him a supportive nod.

Jasper grinned. "Tuck in your tie and grab a pair of gloves." He secured a face shield around Alex's ears.

"What are we doing?" Alex whispered.

"Your first intubation."

Alex's face shield fogged as he straightened. "Am I allowed to do this?"

"Course not," Jasper said, "but you won't get another chance for, what, seven years? All the other pre-meds will be so jealous."

"I don't know, it doesn't feel right."

Jasper sighed. "I'll go first to put your mind at ease. Then I'll walk you through it. See one, do one, teach one."

"I meant, his body. Aren't we defiling it?"

Jasper put up his hands. "I don't want you to do anything you don't want to do. I just thought it would be an interesting experience for you. Go over the anatomy together. He's ninety-five years old, Alex. He lived a long life. Social worker says he doesn't have family."

Greg stood. "These opportunities don't come often. You may want to take advantage."

"Okay, Grandpa." Alex stepped closer to the body.

"I'll leave you to it." Greg exited into the hall and traversed the white tiles. *You're no longer a boy, almost a man.*

The sliding doors of the ambulance bay opened, and Greg stepped out into a light breeze. Perforated bowel in a man who compulsively swallows needles, shattered femur from a gunshot, and a hemorrhagic stroke all in the last two hours. He was going to miss this place. He regarded the façade. Lyons Hospital was awe-inspiring thirty-five years ago when he started as a new attending. Now, white had become beige, with cracks, so many cracks.

The lights in the parking lot turned on with a sizzle, illuminating the helipad in the distance. On slow night shifts, attendings would take residents there to watch the sunrise. It was a beautiful tradition while it lasted. There weren't so many slow nights anymore.

The doors opened behind him. "Sorry to interrupt your daydream honey," Sally called in a tone of practiced condescension, "but I can't find any of the residents. Can you check this EKG?" She handed it to him. "I put him in bed eighteen."

"Of course. How's triage?" He playfully nudged her.

"Don't ask."

Greg's smile faded. "Wow. Not good. I'll see if Jasper wants this one."

"Playing favorites again?" She nudged back.

He rolled his eyes. "Just getting him ready for the next level."

"He's your top resident. He's ready and you know it." She stretched her neck and winced. "Time to head back to the shit tornado. Tell Alex I'll swing by once things settle." Her sneakers squeaked down the hallway.

There were many nurses that Greg had admired over his thirty-five-year span, but Sally was his favorite. She was a spark plug, yet she had soft eyes that could make the hardest gang member feel vulnerable. She had also been a close friend of his wife Linda. He could still hear them cackle over margaritas at his kitchen table; still feel her calming presence next to him upstairs when Linda passed.

"He's a natural." Jasper approached Greg. Alex trailed behind, face pale.

"You okay? Was it too much?" Greg handed Jasper the EKG.

"I'll be fine," Alex said.

Jasper examined the tracing. "Yikes. Any old ones for comparison?"

"Haven't checked," Greg replied. "Bed eighteen."

They walked briskly down the hallway, largely to keep up with Jasper. He had perfected a sprint-walk much to the amusement of the staff. Jasper pulled back the curtain revealing a sweaty patient clutching his chest.

"Please give me something for the pain!"

Greg stayed with Alex and provided the play-by-play.

"Jasper's going to determine how big of an emergency this chest pain is. We already know the electricity in his heart is not normal based on the EKG, and that may be caused by decreased blood flow to his heart. This may be a heart attack, but we'll need some blood tests too. Our goal here is to make sure we don't miss anything else emergent."

Jasper pulled out his stethoscope from a clip on his scrubs and listened to the patient's chest while firing off a series of questions.

"What do you hear?" Greg asked. The blood pressure was 195/105 on the monitor.

"Have you ever been told that you have a heart murmur before?" Jasper asked the patient.

"No." He grunted.

"Sounds like aortic regurg."

"Really?" Greg introduced himself to the patient as the supervising doctor. He listened and nodded in agreement.

"His left radial pulse is weaker than his right," Jasper said.

He squatted next to the patient. "Mr. Collins, your blood pressure is really high, and your EKG is concerning. We need to do some blood work, but first we have to make sure the big blood vessel coming off your heart is okay. We're taking you to the CT scanner now. Do you have an allergy to IV contrast?"

Concern crept into the crevices of the patient's brow. "No ... am I going to die?!"

Jasper gently placed his hand on the patient's arm. "The most important thing you can do is to concentrate on your breathing and try to stay calm. We'll be with you the whole time at the scanner." He turned to the nurse. "Can you give him four of morphine, four of zofran, and prepare ten of labetalol?"

Within minutes they watched the patient slide through the large metal donut of the CT scanner.

"What a day." Jasper scrolled through the images as they uploaded on the screen. "I bet he has it ... only seen it once before."

"I've only had five," Greg said.

"Is this an aortic dissection?" Alex asked. "I read a news article about a famous actor who died from it."

"Check out the rookie. Nice one," Jasper said.

"Very good Alex," Greg said. "The CT scan will tell us for sure."

Their fear materialized. This man needed a surgeon right now. Jasper picked up the phone and dialed. Within thirty minutes the patient was in an elevator to the operating room.

They trekked back to the nurses' station as Alex trailed behind them, speechless.

Greg turned to him. "Jasper just made the diagnosis that saved that man's life," he said. "That's the rush of this job and why I keep coming back."

Alex beamed. "Incredible."

"Dissections are so rare. What a way to start your career!" Greg said. "The key is to control their pain, heart rate, and blood pressure to ..." Greg's words evaporated.

Nurses were amassing outside of room eight.

"Look who woke up," Jasper said.

They joined the horde and Greg stepped in front of Alex. "Try to stay away from this one."

Greg felt him lean around him.

"They're coming here to kill me!" the perched gargoyle shrieked at Peggy.

"Mr. Henderson, please calm down, or we're going to have to give you medication to help you rest," Peggy said.

His icy glare found Jasper, then Greg, and stopped on Alex. A grin crept across his face. "They're coming for you too."

The man's face burned into Greg's retinas.

Alex shuddered as they retreated to the doc box.

"I'm sorry you saw that Alex," Greg said. "We handle emergencies of all kinds including psychiatric ones. Sometimes we keep dangerous people against their will for their own safety and the safety of others."

"And with psychiatric hospitals closing left and right, guess where they come when they finally snap?" Jasper asked.

Greg sat at a computer and opened a chart. "Henderson is one of the evil ones."

Alex reached for the top button of his shirt, noticeably unsettled. "Doesn't he just need the right medication?"

"I've been doing this a long time. Some people, yes, but not him. He's been in and out of psych facilities his whole life. He's destined for a dark path," Greg said.

Sorry to pull the blanket from you, Alex, but here we are. He stole a look at his grandson, who was taking in the room: vacant faces at two rows of computers, keystrokes and clicks, candy, potato chip grease, a "whiteboard of fame" with scribbled lab values, a collective groan as the waiting room jumped from twenty to thirty. *Maybe that's enough for one day.*

Greg walked him to the ambulance bay. "Busiest day of the summer. Have fun?"

"I'll never forget it. Thank you." Alex hugged Greg. He turned toward his car and hesitated. "I can see how hard this job is. To see people at their worst every day ... I really respect you. Hang in there, okay?" He smiled.

Greg returned it. *You have no idea.* "I love you."

Back in the doc box a moment later, Greg's swollen knee was screaming in pain. He dropped heavily onto a chair, pulling out his pocket watch from his white coat. Curious ... it had stopped working. "Jasper, thanks for teaching him today. I know it meant a lot to—"

"RUNNER!" a nurse yelled.

"Code green emergency room, room eight!" the overhead speaker boomed.

"Oh no. Get him!" Greg stood awkwardly. He turned to Peggy. "You didn't sedate him?!"

She flinched. "He was redirectable and calmed—"

"No excuses!" Greg barked.

Nurses and security guards ran through the sliding doors after Henderson.

Greg and Jasper followed, stopping in the ambulance bay. They heard a scream. There were two groups of writhing bodies: security guards with tasers drawn repeatedly firing into a man's back; nurses, huddled on the ground.

"Open a trauma bay!" Sally shouted. The nurses quickly became mobile. They were carrying a limp man as Kate scrambled to hold pressure on his bleeding chest.

Greg saw Sally's face and he knew.

It was Alex.

6. TRAUMA

Her lips were moving, but Greg couldn't hear what she was saying. He couldn't hear anything.

Sally took his face in her hands.

"Greg ... Greg!" Her voice returned with piercing clarity. "Don't go in there. They just paged trauma surgery. Let them handle this. Please!"

Kate was escorted past them, pale and covered in blood.

Greg pulled away. "There's not enough time." He parted the sea of shaken faces and entered the room.

Peggy was frantically assembling her airway equipment at the head of the bed. "Airway is intact! He's moaning!"

Oscar cut off Alex's shirt as Jasper listened to his lungs. "Breath sounds are equal bilaterally. There's a four-centimeter stab wound to the left anterior chest, actively bleeding!" Jasper said, ripping off Alex's shoes and socks to grip his feet. "Guys we need that blood pressure, I have weak pulses here!"

"Blood pressure 82/65, heart rate 120, oxygen saturation 97%!!" Oscar called out.

A cold hand wrapped around Greg's neck. The clanging alarm of the bedside monitor was a death knell. "We need four units of uncrossmatched blood now!" Greg shouted. He grabbed Jasper's shoulder. "Get the thoracotomy tray ready. I'll run this."

"Dr. Bishop, I don't think you—"

"Get it ready now!"

Jasper ran to the cabinet while Greg scanned his chest with the bedside ultrasound. "Heart is contracting. Large pericardial effusion. FAST scan positive!" Greg's shaking hand returned the probe to its holster. *No.* "Alex, keep those eyes open. We're going to take care of you!" He leaned in. "Alex, can you hear me?!"

His head rolled. "Grandpa ..."

"I'm here, I'm here!" Greg choked back tears, grabbing his hand.

"Grandpa ... I don't want to die."

"I won't let that happen." He felt Alex's grip loosen. "Stay with me. Come on Alex, stay with me!!"

"Blood pressure's dropping, 60/40!!" Oscar shouted.

"I don't feel pulses!" Jasper yelled. He splashed betadine on Alex's chest.

"Thoracotomy!" Greg scrambled to put on a gown.

"Proceeding with intubation!" Peggy extended Alex's neck and opened his mouth.

Greg lowered the shaking blade to his grandson's limp body. He took a breath, but his hand didn't move. He turned to Jasper in despair. "I can't cut him."

"Please let me do this." Jasper's eyes locked on Greg. "This needs to happen now."

Greg feebly handed him the blade, then faced the wall and shut his eyes.

"Grandpa." Alex stood at the side of his bed. He must've been eight years old. "I want to give you your Christmas present before anyone else gets one."

Greg opened the box to see his father's pocket watch. I thought I lost this years ago.

"Alex found it in the attic. We cleaned it up for you," Kevin said from the doorway.

My home. My family.

The wall next to Kevin cracked. The fissure deepened and tore through the four walls.

Greg's master bedroom was crumbling.

They're all I have left. Don't take Alex from me!

Fluorescent light from the trauma bay poured in, illuminating young Alex's smile, which morphed into wide-eyed horror as Greg heard his ribs crack open.

Blood splattered on the floor.

"Lots of blood in the left chest!" Jasper said. "Where's trauma surgery? We need them! Peggy, push the tube deeper, right mainstem it."

"Done!" Peggy said. "Good breath sounds on the right side!"

"Massive transfusion protocol. We need four more units of blood, FFP and platelets please!" Jasper's eyes darted around the room. "Dr. Bishop, I need you!"

Greg turned and saw the large gaping hole in Alex's chest. A wave of nausea rushed past his tonsils.

"You've got this," he croaked. "Pack that blood out of the way. How's his lung?"

"Left lung with no obvious trauma. I'm reaching back towards the heart. Okay, I can see it beating ... oh God!"

"What?!" Greg came closer.

"There's a large laceration to the heart!" Jasper grabbed a pair of scissors and cut away the swollen pericardium.

Greg tried to focus as blood squirted out of Alex's right ventricle.

"Suture it. Avoid the coronary arteries." His voice steadied. *This was fixable.*

"Two units of blood in!" Sally said.

Jasper cranked the last stitch tight, sealing it off. He searched inside the chest. "Hemostasis. No other signs of injury."

"Jasper, put in a central line." Greg wiped the sweat from his forehead. "Where's trauma surgery? Overhead alert—"

Alex's heart began contracting wildly.

"He's in Vfib!" Greg grabbed the internal defibrillator paddles. "Set it at thirty joules. Everyone stand back!" Greg leaned forward and gently squeezed Alex's heart with the large, metal spoons. "All—"

His leg buckled. The paddles slid off Alex's heart. The charge deployed. Three lines of elliptical blue light arced between the paddles inside Alex's chest, warping the air in its vicinity. It was radiant, beckoning, and the last thing Greg saw as he crashed down on his decrepit knee.

Floored by the explosive pain, he dragged himself onto a stool in the corner. "Shock him, Jasper!"

"All clear?!" Jasper's shock hit its mark and stunned the chaotic quivering of Alex's heart. The exhausted muscle sputtered, then regained normal contractions.

"I feel pulses," Peggy said.

There was a bustle of activity in the hallway. The trauma surgery team walked briskly into the room.

"We heard the overhead, are the pagers not working?" Dr. Mark Greyson asked, his bloodshot eyes probed Alex's body.

"Mark! Get him upstairs!" Greg said, his sweaty face flushed.

"Are you okay? What happened?!" Mark asked.

Greg grabbed his wrist. "That's my grandson on the table. He was stabbed in the chest!"

"Jesus!"

"I slipped and hit my knee. Mark, that son of a bitch stabbed him in the heart!" A whimper escaped his lips.

Dr. Greyson put his hand on top of Greg's. "We'll take it from here. I'll let you know as soon as we're done." He turned to the room. "Alright let's get him upstairs! Is that bleeding controlled? I need everything portable, let's go!" He pointed at Peggy. "Give me the story on the way up."

Greg watched the caravan fade away. He crumpled against the wall.

Jasper peeled off his gloves and let them fall to the floor. The rest of him followed, and he sat cross-legged next to a crimson puddle. "What just happened? What ... just happened?" He searched for Greg through the fog. "And what was that blue light? Did you see that?"

Sally entered through the curtain, joining them in the trauma bay. Tears streamed down her face. She came to Greg's side and embraced him.

Unable to hold back any longer, he wept.

Twenty minutes passed. Jasper heard an upswell of concerned chatter in the hallway. He summoned the strength to stand. "Shift change ... I think I need to go check—"

The wall phone blared. Greg froze on the blinking white light next to him. He looked at Sally and hit speakerphone.

"Greg?"

"Yes."

"It's Mark. He's alive buddy."

The unbearable tension in his throat released. "Thank you," Greg whispered, his chest heaving.

"You saved him. All we did was give more blood and reinforce your sutures. I'll be up here waiting for you. Whatever you need." Mark hung up.

"Greg, you saved him," Sally said. "Yes, yes, yes. Let's go upstairs!"

Greg smiled weakly, his eyes heavy. "I need a moment."

She gently touched his cheek then clasped her hands toward the ceiling. "Thank you," she mouthed, exiting with Jasper. They closed the curtain. Gasps and hugs spread in the hallway.

Greg sank deeper into the corner. *My Alex. How did I let this happen to you? You almost died in my hands.*

There was no solace in the empty room.

Get up. Do my job. The residents can learn from this. Show them how it's done.

The voice went quiet. It didn't come back.

This was the end of his career.

He had one more thing to do. He picked up the phone and dialed.

"Hello?"

"Kevin, it's Dad ... are you sitting down?"

Test Subject 1
Interaction 3
Ford Hospital
020900SMAY19

Informed Consent for Pneuma Transplant

<u>Today we will be assessing whether you:</u>
[X] Understand the transplant process including the procedural details, risks, benefits, and alternatives
[] Express a choice on whether to proceed consistent with your preferences and values
[] Appreciate the consequences of participating or refusing
[] Show appropriate reasoning when comparing these consequences

[X]: Denotes the objective has been completed
[]: Denotes the objective is still pending

This interaction is being video recorded.

———

"I play chess at a community center near my house with my friend Beatrice." I smile. "Do you play?"

"Unfortunately, I don't have the time," Mr. Montoya replies.

"You should make time. Keeps the mind sharp." I wink. "Let's see ... when I'm not at the center I love a good book."

He leans forward in his chair. "Do you have a favorite genre?"

"I hate to admit it, but I never used to read for pleasure. Nowadays, I like to sample a little bit of everything."

"We're impressed by your curiosity and your thirst for knowledge. It's a large part of why we're interviewing you."

"Thank you, dear."

"That being said." His voice takes a serious tone. "We noticed you left the facility yesterday after our interview." His eyes meet mine. "Where did you go?"

He senses my apprehension. "I don't mean to alarm you, but we've assembled a team here to care for you, and outside these walls we can't ensure your safety unless you alert a member of the staff who can accompany you. Furthermore, please remember we're hoping to learn about you without outside influence from other people."

"I'm so sorry!" I blurt. "It was never my intention to disrupt the study."

He stiffens. "Ms. Trudy, where did you go?"

"Nowhere. I wanted to feel the sun on my skin and have some private time," I lie. "I know I shouldn't do things like that, and it won't happen again. You have my word."

His trademark smile returns. "Good. Thank you for your open communication and I apologize for making you uncomfortable."

He settles into another set of questions as if that little episode never happened, before he excuses me for the day. *We were getting along so well. I hope I didn't make a mess of things.*

I close the door to my room and walk to the window, pausing to catch my breath. I see two small cameras above the entrance of the facility. *Those little tattletales! That's how they saw me leave.* I shouldn't have, but there was a man pacing outside yesterday and he seemed so angry! He struggled to take off his jacket and in the bustle an envelope fell to the ground. He searched frantically, but he couldn't find it. *I had to help him!* I made my way outside only to see him disappear around a corner, still fuming. He mustn't have found it, so I had to try. Luckily, I spotted it lying under a bush.

Wait. With those cameras, Mr. Montoya knew I was outside for only a few minutes, so my safety probably wasn't the issue. I think he was worried I would interact with that man. There was no one else around. He certainly wasn't this upset when I spoke with the janitor the other day.

I recall the man. Dark brown jacket, black hair, and glowering. He's a wild dog cornered in a kennel.

I swell with purpose. *He's the other participant. I'm sure of it. You're why I'm here.*

My revelation quickly sours. If I try to find him, I'll be removed from the study. I sigh and retrieve the envelope from my purse. If this is our only link until the end, so be it. I open it and find a small white card with a handwritten message:

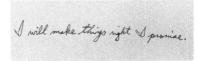

7. WHITE TILES

When Alex was born, Kevin's world exploded with clarity. Colors were brighter and edges sharper. It was as if his own DNA had rewarded him for advancing his species, or maybe it was because he was now seeing for two. He had to keep this beautiful creature alive.

Now, his eyes came back into focus on the monitor next to Alex's bed. Everything was still except for the mechanical rise and fall of his repaired chest. One moment Kevin could breathe, and he almost felt normal, then the darkness and nausea would hit again. He was back on the roller coaster ... *the same one he had prayed he would never have to ride again*: his mother had died two floors above them.

Greg had been intermittently forcing himself awake on a bench by the window. His overnight watch was rapidly deteriorating.

Kevin walked over and stopped cold at the sight of his bloodstains. Alex's blood. "I'll get you new scrubs." He reached for his father's hospital badge.

Greg pulled him onto the seat. "I was supposed to protect him," he groaned. "He's just a boy ... and Henderson, *that demon* ... butchered him."

The account of Alex's attack replayed in Kevin's mind, spiraling him closer to losing all control. He fought away the imagery and the fury screaming to be let loose. "Dad, this isn't your fault," he managed. "There's no way to predict something like that."

"I ran the whole code on him." He looked at Kevin with strangled eyes. "We cracked his chest. We did *everything*."

"Oh God ... no ..."

Twelve years. It took them twelve years of training to approach the human body as if it was a machine. Objectivity. Critical thinking. Systematic desensitization. *But there are no guidelines for when your patient is your grandson and you're drowning in emotion*. The chapters stop there; you just don't do it. It was the worst nightmare of every physician and Kevin understood his father crossed that bridge alone.

They were startled by a knock at the door.

Jasper peeked around the curtain. "Okay if I come in?"

"Yes, of course," Greg said with a confused smile. "What are you still doing here?"

"I slept in the call room. Stuck around in case you needed anything." Jasper placed a set of scrubs on the table. He nodded at Greg.

"You're a good man," Greg said. "This is my son, Kevin. Kevin, this is Jasper, one of our chief residents."

Kevin rose to meet him. They shook hands.

"Pleasure to finally meet you. Dr. Bishop and Sally talk about you all the time. Congratulations on the Chicago Legacy job by the way, it must be nice to be close to home."

Kevin cleared his throat. "Thank you."

The quiet returned, affording Jasper a moment to look at Alex … and the ventilator connected to the tube diving down his throat, breathing for him. He struggled to maintain his composure. "I think I should get going." Jasper excused himself to the door. "I'm really sorry about Alex."

"Stay a little," Greg said. "Kevin, he's been mentoring Alex. He had just taught him how to intubate a few hours ago … Then he was there for it all."

Kevin took a step back. He pulled up a chair for Jasper and rejoined Greg on the bench. "Thank you for saving him."

Jasper sat quietly. "I don't really have the words. Alex is such a good kid, I …" He exhaled. He shifted to the bedside monitor. "Any updates?"

"Not yet," Kevin said. "Pupils are reactive, but he hasn't moved." Saying it out loud took Kevin through another turn, another drop into the black abyss of fear for the worst. He had searched for the sedative drips, but there weren't any. *Alex was in a coma.*

Greg's phone beeped. He shielded it from Kevin, sent a text, and slid it back into his pocket.

Kevin gave him a quizzical look. *I'm guessing that's Susan? You don't have to be secretive, Dad. I called her hours ago.* He turned to Jasper. "What's next after you graduate?"

"I'm thinking about a research fellowship."

"Academic path? Follow in my old man's footsteps."

"He'll be our research fellow next year," Greg interjected.

"We'll see." Jasper laughed uneasily. "There are a lot of rockstar applicants."

"You'll get it." Greg's definitive tone was jarring.

Jasper leaned back, his mouth awaiting a response that didn't come. He rubbed his arm, head lowered.

"Well." Kevin grabbed a plastic cup. "Here's to your coronation."

Jasper followed suit and toasted Kevin, grateful for the levity.

"If you get it, or even if you don't ..." Kevin glanced at his father. "Please contact me anytime. I was a chief too and I know how crazy the transition to the real world can be. I'm happy to be a resource for you." He gave Jasper his business card.

"I will, thank you." He forced a smile and rose to his feet. "I think it's time I go home. Try to rest, Dr. Bishop ... Doctors Bishop." He departed.

Kevin fetched the new scrubs. "Need help changing?"

Greg put his hand on Kevin's shoulder. "Thank you, son. These may be the last ones I wear."

The gravity of his resignation hit Kevin like a truck. He stayed on Greg's somber eyes. His father, the *Lion of Lyons Hospital*, was done.

Kevin slowly exhaled. "I need some air."

"Me too."

Kevin set the new scrubs on the bench and helped Greg into the wheelchair. They made it to the door and opened it.

Susan.

Her eyes swept dismissively over Kevin and targeted Greg. She crouched to his level and gripped his armrests. "What happened to my son?"

They couldn't move. They couldn't speak.

"You're not going to say ... anything?"

Kevin pulled Greg back into the room. Susan stepped forward. She saw Alex.

Her eyes followed the tubes into his arms, into his nose, and into his mouth.

She brushed past the men as if they were shadows on a wall and arrived at Alex's bed. She turned to stone. "You both can leave now."

They silently entered the hallway. Kevin peered over his shoulder and saw her holding their son's hand. Her eyes met Kevin's as the door clicked shut.

8. In His Sights

Kevin knew that look on James's face. He was wondering why he was off.

James sighed and holstered his gun. He turned away from the bullet holes clustered in the target's chest.

Kevin surveyed the dried grass and dirt stretching in all directions. The gun range where they first learned how to shoot was a skeleton of its former self. A mile from a deserted Chicago L Train depot, there were few reminders of the early days left. A rusted metal 'Proceed at Your Own Risk' sign welcomed visitors to both the range and an outhouse, beyond which tired wooden targets leaned in a row parallel with sun-bleached picnic tables.

There he sat with Grace, watching him.

"You're up," James said.

Kevin regarded his unloaded gun, convinced he had chosen the wrong distraction for the day. He was running on his backup generator. The last two days were an all-out assault on his body, mind, and spirit. Even as he made Greg's home wheelchair accessible, he was twisted in frustration by unanswered texts to Susan and smothered by perpetual despair that Alex might never wake up.

"I think I'll just sit for a bit."

"Whatever you need, man."

James glanced at Grace. He grabbed a handful of bullets. "Glad I saw Greg today, been too long."

"He asks about you a lot," Kevin said.

James smiled. "Best Little League coach ever. When's his knee surgery?"

"Two weeks."

In the silence that followed, Grace clearly felt the full weight of Kevin's anguish. She looked at the row of targets searching for the words to comfort him. "You are all stretched so thin. Kevin, this is devastating ... and I'm sorry. I wish I could've been at the hospital with you," Grace said.

He held her gaze. *The train's off the tracks. You don't have to take this on.*

She reached for his hand. *This is where I want to be.*

James finished loading a clip. "I just hope Susan talks to you. Can't hold grudges at a time like this," he said to Kevin.

"I think she'll get there," Grace said. "This is her *son*."

"It's his son too," James said.

"I know. I'm sorry, I'm not trying to make this a competition. I don't know Susan." She bit her lip. "But the way my mom would describe us, her children ... we stay in her core, forever. The bond is overwhelming. Losing Brody almost killed her."

Kevin awoke on the cot next to his mom's hospital bed. There was a car chase on TV, but she wasn't watching it. She had used all her strength to roll onto her side, memorizing his face as he stirred. She reached over and held his hand, her last moment of lucid, pure love.

Kevin nodded. "She's probably still in shock."

James offered the clip to Grace. She smiled and shook her head. "I haven't since basic training. No more guns for me."

James pulled back in disbelief. "Wow, you bled Navy blue … until there wasn't a drop of Navy left." He stood and loaded his gun, pausing before putting it in the holster.

"It's not the Navy. It's just guns." Grace looked him over. "Anything else on your mind?"

Down the path, James's target sheet flapped in the wind. He felt a chill. "Once I heard about Alex I had to come back, but there's something else, yeah." He straddled the bench across from them. "Sticks, remember that slacker student I told you about? He also failed a written exam, and someone changed his score. I reported it, and the next thing I know I'm being investigated."

"What?" Grace pressed forward on the table. "For doing your duty?"

"He's the nephew of the commanding officer," Kevin said.

He saw something in James's face he'd never seen before. Uncertainty.

Grace held her breath. "Captain's Mast?"

"Worse. Court-martial in a few weeks."

Her jaw dropped. "On what grounds?!"

"Unlawful entry."

Grace steadied herself. Her jaw reset. "What did you do?" she whispered.

"Remember who taught you how to pick a lock? I broke into the CO's office to find his test. I had to be sure."

Kevin saw the mission play out in his head. Nighttime, under five minutes, no noise, everything where it should be. "But you're a ghost, there's no way they'd know you were there unless—"

"I was ratted out." James spun a bullet on the table and slammed it. "I spoke with another teacher, Kaminsky, about the test. A close friend. He's the only one I thought I could trust. The way he looked at me after ... I know his tell. They must have something on him too."

"You can fight this. You're a legend in Coronado and you've been overseas twice," Grace said. "I know your character and I'm a professional reference. Use me."

"I may have to. Not many left in my corner." James stood.

"Who's your commanding officer?" she asked.

"William Kedge. He actually goes by William. What a self-entitled asshat. A real prick. The ambitious type who would run over his mother to get ahead."

"I'll reach out to Brody's friends, see what I can find," she said.

"I already asked them." James turned and walked towards the target.

Kevin's cloud lifted as his focus shifted to his lifelong friend. He stood and loaded his gun. "I have to go talk to him. I know he's glad you're in his corner." He slid the earmuffs back on Grace's head and kissed her nose.

"Anything for my boys!" she yelled over the ear-protector's mute.

Kevin found James sizing up the target.

He drew and fired. "Fuck." James spit.

Kevin tapped him. "Is your right shoulder hurting?"

"The point of today was to get you out of the hospital, not bring it here."

"Just watching your back, Dowd."

"You always do," James said. Another bullet blasted out of his pistol. His arm fell to his side. He rotated it slowly. "Yeah, it's stiff."

"Might be why you're low. Your left hand's sliding under to compensate. Switch hands?"

James snickered. He flipped the gun to his left hand and shot. "You're right."

Kevin studied the target. "How do you figure? You missed."

"You sure?" James grinned.

Kevin walked over and pulled it off the frame. In the corner was a small black dot with a bullet hole in its center.

Test Subject 2
Interaction 5
Ford Hospital
021300SMAY19

Informed Consent for Pneuma Transplant

<u>Today we will be assessing whether you:</u>
[X] Understand the transplant process including the procedural details, risks, benefits, and alternatives
[] Express a choice on whether to proceed consistent with your preferences and values
[] Appreciate the consequences of participating or refusing
[] Show appropriate reasoning when comparing these consequences

[X]: Denotes the objective has been completed
[]: Denotes the objective is still pending

This interaction is NOT being video recorded.

"Why are we still in this bullshit room? I've agreed to the procedure," I say.

He slowly adjusts his cufflinks. The other interviewer couldn't sit still and this one's acting like he's on Xanax, straight out of a men's fall catalogue. I check around him. No briefcase. No folders.

"You've agreed, and you know the risks, benefits, and alternatives, but when we ask you *why* you feel you need it, you give rote answers like 'because I need it.' For something of this magnitude, we need more thoughtful—"

"You need to know if I have the capacity to make my decision."

He takes a moment, inspecting me. He nods.

Yeah, I know my shit, clown. "You guys have been dicking around with photos and mind games."

"They're afraid of you. They don't know the best approach."

"And you do?" I grin.

He shrugs.

"You're not afraid of me, huh?" I lock onto his eyes.

He leans forward to give me a better view. "No."

The tail of a black scorpion slides up above his collar. "Cute neck tattoo. I only see those on women who like to be choked."

"Sounds like a good match for a bad boy like you."

"They serve their purpose. They keep my dick wet and give me the little money they have."

"And now you sit across from me, who can give you neither."

I move closer. "I'll find a use for you."

He's still. A smile appears. "Well, you are very resourceful." He leans back. "While I admire your toughness, it's gotten you into trouble: theft, violent acts. Then, something brought you here. That's the part of you I need to meet."

"The last interviewer didn't get very far. Good luck."

"Fuck that guy. I don't like him either," he says.

I search his face. *Trying to switch teams and join mine?*

"Per 'informed consent guidelines,' your decision to proceed needs to be congruent with your preferences and values. So, my first goal is to see if you know yourself," he says. "When you look inside, what do you see?"

I stare past my scarred knuckles. "Locked doors."

"Must be hard."

"What's hard is that I remember everything. I know what it all felt like before. Now, I'm just like them." I glance dismissively at the mirror. "Watching from a distance."

"No one's observing today. I asked for that."

"And another thing, I don't trust anyone."

"Come see then?" He stands. "Let me show you."

Another test? See how I handle stress with my guard down?

I enter the hallway and see a security guard. He's the one who slammed his knee into my back. I glare at him.

My interviewer signals it's okay. He scans his badge and opens a door. No camera, no voyeurs getting off to our talk.

As we walk back, I approach the guard, who stiffens against the wall. "Not so easy when your friends aren't around," I mock. "You're a fucking rent-a-cop, Lowry."

His hand hovers near his nightstick.

"Do it." I tap my chin.

Lowry grabs his belt. He jerks away, teeth clenched.

"Run little doggy." I watch him leave.

We return to the interrogation room. He closes the door and relaxes in his chair. "Tell me more. What's important to you?" he asks.

My hand instinctively reaches inside my empty jacket pocket. *The most important thing in my life was made of paper. My card. How pathetic.*

9. CASTLE BISHOP

Through his frosted breath, Greg could see inside the crushed Chrysler LeBaron where his mother and sister were entombed. His shaking flashlight found a trail of blood, then another body. His father lay face down in the snow. The only thing Greg could save was his father's pocket watch, a gift from his best friend when Greg was born thirty years before. His eyes fell on an engraving on the back:

YOU ONLY HAVE SO MUCH
TIME WITH HIM

MAKE IT COUNT

Kevin quietly observed his father from the kitchen doorway. Greg was in his wheelchair, staring out the window, muttering to himself. "He was having trouble seeing at night. I could have stopped him from driving. I could have prevented it." He rocked. "I could have sedated Henderson. I could have prevented it."

"Hey."

His father flinched. He turned to Kevin, emerging from a haze.

"Want to get out of it for a while? Lie down?" Kevin asked.

He thumbed the cheap leather. "No."

"Don't worry Professor, you'll be back leading the X-men in no time."

Greg searched for something to throw. "You're lucky I can't stand. I'd have you on your back so fast, little boy."

He began his low-speed chase.

Kevin grinned and backpedaled into the living room.

Greg clipped a cupboard and yelped. His hand darted to his knee. He probed it. "I hate this fucking thing!" He slammed the armrests.

Kevin approached with caution. He freed the stuck wheel and rolled him back to the kitchen table. "All of this is temporary. Things will go smoothly once the caregiver comes tomorrow. She sounds great, lots of experience."

"Caregiver," Greg scoffed. "Next thing I'll be one of those comatose idiots on a park bench feeding ducks."

"Please don't make this more difficult than it needs to be. The new security cameras wouldn't have anything to do with her, would they?"

Greg shifted. "Jasper set them up. She's a stranger in my home. I want to be safe."

Kevin bit his tongue. There were some battles worth fighting, but this was not one of them. "Grace will be here soon. Are you in any shape to meet her?"

Greg's eyes widened. "I must have forgotten. Fucking opiates are making my head fuzzy." He slowly nodded before shaking his head. "Probably not the best time. I should lie down."

Kevin assumed his position behind Greg and pushed him forward.

The doorbell rang.

They stopped. Greg slumped. "I really didn't want her to see me like this."

"She doesn't care about appearances."

"I do."

Kevin cracked opened the door. "Hi, baby, I don't think Dad's feeling too well—"

"She can come in."

Grace entered with a smile, saying, "Hi," with grocery bags in tow.

Greg regarded her, confused.

"Meet my dad and move in on the same day? You work fast." Kevin kissed her cheek and took the bags.

Grace rolled her eyes before directing them at his father. "Kevin mentioned some of your favorite things, so I made a pit stop. Hope that's okay."

Greg's facial muscles contorted into his first smile of the week. "Very thoughtful, thank you."

She leaned in and hugged him. "Nice to meet you. I can't believe you like speculoos too. Not many people know about it."

"Gooey cinnamon. It's the best." Greg warmed up. "You know a way to a man's heart."

Through his pancreas, Kevin thought. *With more weight on his crumbling knee.* He unloaded the cargo in the kitchen.

Grace pointed to the photo from Kevin's white coat ceremony. "That's amazing."

"Did you tell her?" Greg asked proudly.

Kevin finished loading eggs into the refrigerator. "I had just started USC med school a few months before, and I was homesick. Dad said he couldn't make it, so it was a rough morning, seeing everyone celebrating with their families. Then, when it was my turn on stage, he came out from behind the curtain with my white coat."

"What a great surprise." Grace smiled. "It must be nice to have a shared path."

"No one else in medicine in your family?" Greg asked.

"Just me," Grace said.

"That's really special." Greg leaned forward. "To create a career for yourself on your own. It makes accomplishments that much sweeter."

Kevin's hand stopped in the final bag of groceries. *Unless that career's in music, then I get pushed into medicine, right Dad? Hypocrite.*

Grace went to Kevin's side. "It's such a tough road no matter what. I'm just grateful to do what I do at the end of the day."

Kevin finished unpacking. "Let's get you ready for bed, Dad."

He wheeled him to his makeshift bed in the guestroom. After a chorus of grunts and halting stumbles, Greg was transferred to the mattress. Kevin stretched upright, fighting the spasm in his lower back.

Greg's phone vibrated on the bedside table. He opened a text. "Susan updated UCLA about Alex," Greg said. "They froze his enrollment and financial aid."

Kevin closed his eyes. Fall quarter was coming up in two weeks. This would be a huge year for Alex. Biology and organic chemistry. *Shit.* That goal seemed light-years away. "Anything else?"

"That was my only text from her."

Please, Susan. Talk to me, not my dad. This is hard enough already. Kevin mulled over the words he wanted to text but didn't.

They said their goodnights. Kevin turned off the light and shut the door.

"We should leave soon," Grace said. "I just need to grab something from my car." She disappeared behind the click of the front door.

Get horizontal. Kevin sprawled on the carpet. He felt a twinge near his spine, then some relief. Maybe shut his eyes for a moment ...

"Kevin, why are you just sitting there?" His father was above him, surrounded by his residents. "Beds one to twelve are yours, what's taking so long? You haven't seen any of them!"

He tried to stand but he couldn't move; he was glued to the chair.

"Get up! You're embarrassing me."

The speaker above him crackled to life. "Code blue, bed eleven!"

That's Mom's voice.

And that's Alex's room.

Kevin struggled frantically to escape his confinement. The skin of his forearms stretched against the faux leather armrests to the point of tearing.

"Dad, help Alex! He's dying!"

His father turned to Alex's room in unison with his residents. The row of white coats stood with their backs to Kevin, staring at the flashing alarms as the nurses were desperately waving for their assistance.

"But that's your room," Greg said.

Kevin strained to stand with all his might, as his fear boiled over into explosive rage. "Do something!" He ripped his arms off the chair.

Kevin startled awake, his arms lying listlessly at his sides. Searching the room in confusion, he saw Grace sitting on the couch. "How long did I ..."

"Two hours," she said.

"Two hours?" He checked his watch. "I'm so ..."

"You needed to rest." She sat next to him and gently rubbed his concerned face. "Don't worry about it."

He sighed.

"Nightmare again?" she asked.

He nodded.

"Alex?"

"Every time."

The concern transferred to Grace's face for a moment. She helped him up. "Want to go outside? We aren't going to see many more warm nights."

They made their way to the backyard. Grace stopped under the golden light. "Building a deck?" she asked.

He nodded, head down, feet in the shadow of the eaves. "Summer project for me and Alex."

She moved to him. "Maybe I can watch you two finish it? I'll take notes."

He brought her in close.

"Kevin." She placed her hands on his chest. "I'm proud of you. You've been so strong."

He broke eye contact.

"Hey." She intercepted his gaze. "I never want to add to your hardships. We can be as light as you need right now." She reached into her pocket and handed him two tickets. "We weren't going to the play tonight. I thought more distraction could help, but it wasn't the right one. Cubs game. Surprise."

He was stunned. *She gets me.* He was entranced by the soft light on her skin. "You're my person."

"Yeah?" She beamed.

"Yeah." He looked at his watch. "We still have time."

"The game will be halfway over."

"I thought I'd have a plan for after the theater, so I booked us a table at Petrulli's." He led her back inside. "Thank you for the game, that was so thoughtful. I love the Cubs, but I'd rather look at you." He kissed her deeply and for a moment it all melted away. They didn't even hear his phone signal a text had come in.

She beat him to the front door, both filled with the same excitement as their first date. He grabbed his keys, and then his phone's reminder alert reached him.

The text was from Susan:

He opened his eyes

10. ICU

"Do you think he's in pain?" Susan picked her fingernail.

"I don't know."

Alex's changes were subtle. Cracked lips and patchy facial hair circled the tube in his throat, while his fixed eyes now stared beyond the ceiling with an occasional blink. His surroundings were markedly different. Flowers filled the room. Susan's command station was set up amongst the machines near his head.

She grabbed her fork.

"You're no better than that clueless trauma team." Her bare ring finger came into view, as she stabbed at the untouched lump of food on her tray. "How many years did you go to school again?"

Kevin deflected her daggers. After ten minutes of failing to communicate with his son, they were the least of his worries. He stood. "There's a saying in medicine, 'Don't just do something, stand there.' Sometimes you have to wait."

"Since when is waiting your specialty?" The large vein swelled in the middle of her forehead like the hood of a viper protecting her young. "*I waited.* Waited while you spoke with that fucking therapist every week, only for you to sit across from me, silent, at the dinner table."

A flood of memories, of arguments, of years of miscommunication and hurt rushed through Kevin, drowning his concern for Alex. He was on the defense again with Susan, pushed back against the ropes of his ego. Her mere presence triggered autonomic responses, and he couldn't hold himself back. "Every time I tried to talk to you, you'd rip my head off. I felt like I was at work twenty-four-seven."

"Couples disagree. It requires work," she said. "You quit."

"What choice did I have? You wouldn't come to therapy with me. It was as if we were speaking different languages."

"Yeah, you weren't speaking."

Kevin turned away and walked to the window. "I had nothing left to give you. I had to do what was best for me."

"At the expense of your fam—"

"Us."

She shoved her food aside. "What did I do that was so terrible?! I made a living, I cooked, I fucked you, and your family loved me."

"Great on paper, right?"

"Yes!" She threw up her hands.

"Just on paper."

Her hands fell.

"We've been over this. Your obsession with control. The micromanaging and judging," Kevin said. "I stood by for too long and watched you treat Alex the same way. I had a shred of hope things might change once he went off to college, but then you doubled down on me."

"I was just trying to bring out the best in both of you. Is that a bad thing? I helped him get into his first choice for college and let's not forget you and medical school!"

He gripped the window ledge. "You can change behavior, but you can't change the *person.* Did you ever want the real me, or just the version you tried to mold me into?"

"Start by looking in the mirror." She glared at him. "Two-way street."

His hand unclenched. He lowered himself onto the bench.

"You're really gone, aren't you?" she asked.

"I moved back to Chicago."

The air squeezed out of Susan's lungs. She winced.

It had been a year since their divorce; even though her words were often hostile, Kevin knew Susan was leaving the door open for him. She was holding onto hope for a future together, but there was only one way for them both to heal and grow. There had to be closure. Finality.

Kevin hated hurting anyone, let alone someone he'd shared half his life with; someone who meant so much to him, but it had to be done.

She turned to the bed. Her voice seeped out from her shielded face. "Did you tell him?"

"Yes."

She nodded, wiping away a tear. "Did you do it to be with someone?" she whispered.

"No, I'm just trying to get a new start." He hesitated. "But I met someone."

A strand of her blonde hair fell across her cheek. It quivered. "Do I know her?"

He shook his head.

"Name?"

"Grace."

"Of course, it is," she muttered. "Bask in each other's self-righteousness." Susan's head fell back against the wall. She stared at the yellow, sagging ceiling tiles before lowering her gaze into the dark bathroom. "I can't believe I'm back in this shithole."

"I know," Kevin said. "Mom left us twenty years ago."

Her vein receded. She stood with her full plate of food and dumped it in the trash. "And they still haven't changed the menu."

Kevin regarded her narrowing waistline with concern. "I hope you're taking care of yourself."

Susan let out an exasperated laugh. "I need a good night's sleep. I need a shower. But I don't need this cafeteria garbage." She sat and adjusted her pencil skirt. "Where was Linda's room again? Upstairs?"

"Yeah. 412."

"That's right. You could see the airport." She folded her cardigan tightly across her chest, glancing at the bedside table. "I remember her little notes to the nurses. If she knew they were angry or sad she'd draw cartoons to cheer them up, with silly quotes in thought bubbles."

"Yes. My other favorite memory was walking in on your dance party."

Susan reddened. "Gloria Gaynor, 'I Will Survive.' Linda was too weak to walk, but she could still boogie."

Mom never lost that side of her, even after her endless procedures.

"It meant a lot to me that you were there. To them too."

"You could hardly keep your head up, for months. It was so hard to reach you, but I kept trying." Her voice trailed off. "I trusted things would get better and they did. For a long time."

He met her look. "And I will always be grateful for that. Thank you."

She opened her mouth, then it slowly closed. She reached into her pocket. "Are things serious with Grace?"

Kevin took a deep breath. His hands slid down his thighs. "I think so. She's with Dad now. She'd really like to visit Alex at some point, Susan."

Susan closed her eyes. She didn't move.

"I ..."

She reached out her closed fist. He hesitated, then slid his hand under hers. Her wedding ring landed in his palm.

Test Subject 1
Interaction 4
Ford Hospital
030900SMAY19

Informed Consent for Pneuma Transplant

<u>Today we will be assessing whether you:</u>
[X] Understand the transplant process including the procedural details, risks, benefits, and alternatives
[] Express a choice on whether to proceed consistent with your preferences and values
[] Appreciate the consequences of participating or refusing
[] Show appropriate reasoning when comparing these consequences

[X]: Denotes the objective has been completed
[]: Denotes the objective is still pending

This interaction is being video recorded.

———

I check my oxygen tank. *The air feels thick. I think I need my inhaler. I would hate to ruin my lipstick, though.*

Mr. Montoya looks up from his paperwork. "Are you okay, Ms. Trudy?"

I straighten and pull the sleeves of my sweater over my hands. "I'm a little off, it seems, but nothing I can't manage, dear."

His leg shakes under the table. "Would you like the medical staff to evaluate you?"

I cover my mouth and clear my throat to hide a cough. "Oh, I don't want to cut our time short. I'm happy to continue." I nod pleasantly at the ghosts behind the mirror, who have yet to introduce themselves.

He's not convinced, reluctantly changing the topic. "You've been through so much in your life. What do you value now? What sustains you?"

"Besides my oxygen tank?" I laugh.

He nods nervously. *Poor thing, he's so concerned.*

"Friends. I didn't really have any, before, and I somehow convinced myself that being alone was necessary to reach the pinnacle of my field. As I see it now, I can't fathom how I felt that way. It's a shame. But I was given a second chance and I believe people deserve them. Also, honest connection with others. Compassion and empathy."

There's his smile.

"Admirable." He scribbles on his paper.

It's so quiet here, I can literally hear him write. Music. That's what this place needs. Maybe I'll ask for a radio for my room tonight.

"I'd like to transition to a few questions regarding the trauma you experienced. According to the medical records your heart stopped during your resuscitation. When you awoke, did you think you had changed because of a spiritual awakening?"

"I didn't know how or why I had changed then. All I knew is that I felt at peace with it."

"Did you find God?"

"I found some really good doctors. God and I have always kept a respectful distance from one another. That's one thing that hasn't changed."

"So, you wouldn't consider yourself religious ..."

"Not formally, but I believe in the strength of a loving community."

I exhale and hear a familiar whisper. Then again, louder. The wheeze triggers a wave of coughs that barrel up my throat. I reach for my handkerchief and catch it.

Blood.

11. OVERCAST

Alex was underwater, floating in black hues. He turned and felt pain in his lower lip. His eyes searched. There was nothing around him. He moved his head again, same result. *What's happening?* He slowly tested his fingers and toes; the pain-free movement brought relief. Maybe if he kept his head still, he could swim. He moved his arm—

A spear covered in barbed wire twisted the left side of his chest. He clamped his arm on the searing pain. In his struggle, he failed to notice another change occurring. He was moving upwards, towards light. He breached the surface and gasped, as air filled the dormant nooks in his lungs. He was under an empty, grey sky. No land in sight, just ocean.

"Can you hear me? It's Mom. I'm here. Everyone's here!"

Alex's eyes rolled off their fixed axis. He squinted in the bright, blurry room.

"How's my guy?" Kevin's voice cracked.

Alex ran his tongue over a cut in his lower lip. He sluggishly moved his fingers and toes, clearly aching from inactivity.

"I'm weak," he said. He was hesitant to move his arm.

"We love you so much." Susan smoothed his raven hair. "You've been through a lot."

Alex registered each person in the room, pausing on his grandfather in his wheelchair. His confusion increased when he saw a stranger in the room. "Who are you?"

Dr. Greyson stepped forward from the corner. "Hi. I'm Mark. Nice to meet you. Your Grandpa Greg has been a friend of mine for a long time." He leaned over his bed. "Are you comfortable?"

Alex took a shallow breath. "If I don't move."

"Would you like pain medicine?"

His eyes moved towards a mounted TV in the corner. "I don't know."

"Honey don't be afraid to say what you need," Susan said.

He stared at the blank screen.

Dr. Greyson followed his stare for a moment. "You can let me know at any point if you want some." He smiled. "I'm going to ask you a few silly questions now. Is that okay?"

"Yes."

"Can you tell me your name?"

He searched the depths. "Alex."

"Can you cough for me?"

He tried and grimaced. "Hurts."

Dr. Greyson nodded. "It will be uncomfortable for a few days. Alex, do you know where you are?"

"Hospital."

"Which one?"

Alex was met with optimistic nods, then he saw Greg, whose face was ashen.

"Lyons. I was with grandpa." He paused, before his right hand crept across his chest. He felt bandages and pulled away.

"And I was with you too. We've been here for the last five days," Dr. Greyson said.

"Five days?" Alex drifted to the stranger's badge. *Trauma surgery.*

The room disappeared.

He was in the parking lot, sprawled on the pavement. It was a black-and-white silent film. A distorted face with wild eyes above him. A shard of glass coated with his blood.

"He stabbed me," Alex whispered.

"He's gone!" Greg croaked. "They arrested him. He's gone forever. You're safe."

"He stabbed me," Alex repeated. The words felt foreign, as if someone else was saying them. They didn't register.

Empty, grey sky. No land in sight, just ocean. Alex's hazel eyes found his mother. "I can't feel anything."

12. SHELL

Kevin watched from a bench outside the entrance to Lyon's Hospital, as ash from a patient's lit cigarette blew backwards into his own face. Cursing, he stomped the cigarette with his bare foot, grabbed his IV pole and scurried past, his gown only partially covering his furry butt.

Kevin blinked. "Sometimes I really miss county hospitals."

"This one's charming, to say the least." Grace viewed the stained entryway's chipped columns; the perched pigeons looked back at her, comfortable. "But how cool is your new hospital? I mean seriously."

He nodded.

"Plus, Chicago Legacy's pretty close to a certain someone." She smiled.

"My favorite perk." They interlaced fingers; he kissed her hand. "How was your day?"

She leaned back on the bench. "I've had an elderly patient with dementia all week. He was unbearable ... barking orders, very aggressive ... but he was just scared. He knew he was dying, alone. When he finally wore himself out, I joined the doc and the chaplain, and we all held hands with him. We stayed with him until the end. To see him find relief in his last moments was so moving. It was beautiful."

"That's a powerful thing to share," Kevin said.

"That's what excites me. Reaching out to help people when they're at their worst, and finding a way in." She kissed his hand. "But you know what I'm talking about."

"Yes." He smiled at her.

"We have incredible jobs."

"And I'm so grateful we found each other."

She smiled back, absorbing his warmth.

Another patient came into view on a bench next to them, wearing the familiar hospital gown. He was young, maybe in his twenties, his bandaged face a mix of fear, and flickers of anger at his misfortune.

"Kevin." Grace exhaled slowly. "I never told you this, but I was an ER nurse at trauma centers when I was active duty in the Navy."

Kevin's brow furrowed with questions.

"After nursing school, I was assigned to Iraq and Afghanistan for most of my four-year deployment. And I saw … a lot." Her voice wavered. "I'm so sorry, this is not the right time."

Kevin sat with her. "It's okay. You can tell me."

She looked at him hesitantly.

"Please," he said.

"My … patients came from both sides of the war, but they were all the same. They were young, healthy, full of life, and then they were changed forever. The ones caught in gunfire shook me the most. Guns. That's a whole different kind of hurt. Body after body torn apart beyond recognition … like my brother."

There were no words.

"I just … want you to understand me." Grace stood.

Kevin joined her, slipping his arm around her waist. "Thank you."

"Let's go see your boy."

Kevin nodded, slow to move. "I hope this trauma hasn't changed Alex too. Physically, he'll be okay, but emotionally, I'm not sure. He was not himself yesterday, almost unrecognizable."

"It's early." Grace gave a supportive smile. "He's recovering."

"Yeah."

They fell in step together until they passed through the metal detectors and entered the lobby. The halls were lined with despondent faces and festering wounds. The air was stale. They chose the stairs.

Grace slowed in front of him. "I think I'll go down the hall to the waiting room."

He stopped her on the stair above him. "Is this too much for you today?"

"With everyone on edge, worried about Alex, I don't know," she said.

"I don't know what we're walking into either," Kevin said. "But Dad was asking about you. You made quite the first impression."

She nodded. "I'm just glad to be here to support you."

"Susan … might be a little hostile, but she's harmless."

They entered the hallway and were engulfed by a navy-blue procession. Nurses clustered around a janitor who was attending to something on the floor. Dr. Greyson was with Susan on the other side of the crowd. Greg was being wheeled in the opposite direction. Then Kevin smelled it.

"Mrs. Bishop? I hear—"

"Susan," she corrected him.

"I hear you," Dr. Greyson restarted, as his residents tried to disappear into the wall behind him. "With extreme trauma like this, we've seen people react in varied ways. Plus, he's confused because he's on pain medication—"

"The painkillers again! Alex has taken opiates before and never behaved like this. He just crapped on the floor and kept walking. Don't you think I know my own son?" Her face flushed. "That stranger in there wants nothing to do with us."

"Please give us—"

"Get a psychiatrist, or I'll find one myself."

Kevin turned to Grace, but she was already on the other side of the nurse's station departing with the trauma team. "Waiting room," she mouthed.

He parted the blue sea and approached Susan.

Her arms folded. "Something's wrong with him and no one's taking it seriously."

"I just heard."

"Not only this." She gestured toward the floor. "Everything about him is different."

"In what way? Even more distant?" Kevin asked.

"I don't know how to describe it." She shook her head helplessly.

"I'll go talk to him."

"Good luck. He doesn't want to see anyone."

Kevin knocked on the doorframe. "It's Dad. Can I come in?"

Alex's back was to him. He was standing, staring out the window. He turned and peered at Kevin through disheveled hair.

"What you're going through must be so hard. I'm here for you. We all are."

"I see that." His son moved slowly to the edge of the bed.

Kevin came closer. "Are you okay?"

Alex's brow rippled. "I don't think so."

"What's wrong?" Kevin asked.

His breathing was slow, automatic. "There's nothing."

"If there's nothing wrong, that's good, right? You just—"

"No. There's nothing here."

Kevin searched for his meaning. "Feeling detached?"

Alex nodded.

"I've been there," he said. "Feeling like you're in a dream. Outside looking in."

"Not like this." Alex looked at his sallow skin. His muscles were losing definition.

Kevin wiped his sweaty palms on his jeans. "Have you eaten today?"

"Don't want to. Pointless," Alex said.

"Pointless? You need it to heal. Stay strong."

"You sound like them. You should leave."

"Don't want to." Kevin smiled.

Alex climbed into bed, his back facing his father.

Kevin nodded to himself. He went to the corner and sat next to a pile of untouched books. He picked up the ukulele he'd brought that morning and tested a few notes. Alex had tuned it perfectly in the backyard. *When they were all home, together.* Kevin's hand slid over the polished wood before he plucked the opening solo of the Eagles' 'Hotel California.' They would listen to it after every swim meet. It was tradit—

"I would prefer silence," Alex said.

A cold dread spread around Kevin's heart.

A knock at the door pulled him away from his fear. Dr. Carolina Cruz breezed in and introduced herself as the psychiatrist the hospital assigned to assess Alex. Kevin introduced himself, they shook hands, and she asked for some privacy. He obliged and sought refuge from his anxiety in the waiting room where Grace stood.

He had to sit. His legs were weak.

"What are you thinking, baby?" She eased into the chair next to him. "How is he?"

"He's vacant, all of him, and he's not getting better. I can't see Alex in there, Grace."

"Hopefully this is still part of his healing process, right? Are you worried about something else, like mental illness?"

Kevin held his head in his hands. *It must be from the trauma. Nothing else makes sense. Maybe depression? Catatonia? But he isn't delusional or hallucinating, and aside from anxiety, mental illness didn't run in Alex's bloodline.* He managed a drained shrug.

Their phones chirped. A text from James:

They court-martialed Kaminsky too. Trumped-up charge. They're cleaning house. Miss you guys. Sending love

"Oh God, I feel horrible," Grace said. "The only thing I found on William Kedge is that his whole family tree is military. Dad's a senator, too."

"That's probably why you haven't found any dirt." Kevin sighed. "You care, and you tried. That's all that matters to James, you know that."

"I just wish there was something we could do."

"I like his odds. I can't think of a better person to face a judge. Once he turns on that charisma ..."

Grace shook her head. "He's a decorated Navy SEAL and they're throwing him under the bus." She heard voices in the hall and stood. "I should go. Please call me later." They hugged and parted with a deep kiss. It held a promise. Every time.

Greg and Susan soon arrived with Dr. Cruz. She was catching up with Greg, whom she'd known since they joined the faculty at the hospital the same year. She quickly felt Kevin and Susan's impatience and shifted into professional mode, sitting across from them.

"I had a very interesting discussion with Alex. Greg, I witnessed the detachment you're referring to. I was not able to elicit an emotional reaction at all."

"He's normally very engaging," Kevin said. "He's never been like this. Do you think it's from the trauma?"

"Most likely, yes. Being emergency doctors, I'm sure you and Greg can attest that people react to stressors differently. Adjustment disorder, PTSD are possibilities," Dr. Cruz said, "but what's interesting is that even when people suppress painful experiences, the trauma finds ways to infiltrate during the day or during sleep. Alex, on the other hand, seems profoundly apathetic to everything."

"Could there be something else wrong with him?" Susan asked.

"I don't have a clear answer yet. We need more time."

Greg wheeled closer.

"Oh, I know that look," Dr. Cruz said.

"And Carolina, I know you." Greg reached for her hand.

She received it, glancing up at a photo of an island hanging behind him.

"There are other diagnoses you're considering," Greg said.

Condensation beaded on her thick rimmed glasses. "It's unprofessional to speculate this soon after he regained consciousness."

"We're past professionalism. This is my family. Please. Speculate," Greg said.

Carolina slid her hand back and sat upright. "I … know this may sound bizarre, maybe even far-fetched, but there are some troubling elements of schizoid personality disorder, particularly where people prefer isolation, and have difficulty experiencing deep or lasting emotion."

Greg seemed as confused as Kevin.

"But personality disorders persist throughout a lifetime," Kevin said. "This is all new."

"Are you saying his personality changed?" Susan picked the scab along her fingernail.

"I don't know. Again, we need more time. But his ability to eat or care for himself is impaired. I'm going to place him on a psychiatric 5150 hold. He won't—"

"What?" Kevin exclaimed.

"Carolina, please. Not that. There must be another option," Greg said.

"I'm so sorry. This might be short-term." She turned to a bewildered Susan. "But this means he won't be able to leave the hospital. I spoke with Dr. Greyson. He plans to medically clear Alex tomorrow, and then he'll be transferred to a psychiatric facility."

Susan went still. "You're taking him from us, and you don't know why?"

"You'll be able to visit, every day, and there will be ongoing assessments. You'll have an answer soon."

"Greg, I need a moment with you. Thank you, Dr. Cruz, that'll be all."

Carolina nodded and quietly left.

"I can't take much more of this. Oh fuck," Susan whispered. "Greg, do you trust Dr. Cruz? Is she a good psychiatrist?"

Greg rubbed his armrests, appearing nauseous. "One of the best."

Susan's lip quivered. She scanned the sets of downward eyes, placing her hand on Greg's good knee. "I know we haven't talked about what you did in the ER, but is there something you're not telling us?"

Kevin watched Greg's eyes careen through his tortured memories.

Then his father stopped breathing. "No."

Test Subject 2
Interaction 6
Ford Hospital
031300SMAY19

Informed Consent for Pneuma Transplant

<u>Today we will be assessing whether you:</u>
[X] Understand the transplant process including the procedural details, risks, benefits, and alternatives
[] Express a choice on whether to proceed consistent with your preferences and values
[] Appreciate the consequences of participating or refusing
[] Show appropriate reasoning when comparing these consequences

[X]: Denotes the objective has been completed
[]: Denotes the objective is still pending

This interaction is being video recorded.

The door opens and Mr. Men's Fall Catalogue enters in a turtleneck and pea coat. *Of course, he would.*
I hear running in the hall.
"We need more breathing treatments. Call Travis!" a man yells.
He shuts the door quickly.

"What's going on?" I smirk.

His game face returns, joining me at the table. "Sorry, no details."

"Someone's pretty sick," I say. "The other subject?"

"Not going to happen. The focus needs to stay on you."

"But I'm so boring. Out there, that's excitement. Is he dying?"

He slides off his coat. "I want to revisit—"

"Is he dying?"

His mouth tightens. "Can I stick to asking the questions? Please?"

That's right, beg. "I just hope your team knows what to do. Wouldn't look good for him to die. Might throw a wrench into this whole thing."

"She'll be fi ..." The words catch in his throat.

I lean in. "She?"

His eyes search for a place to land.

The other test subject's a woman. Are you kidding me?

"I'll be right back." He pushes up from the table.

We're in the final moments and now this shit? How would that even work?!

The door opens and he exits. Lowry enters. I stand and try to focus on him, but my head's spinning. I target his disgusting zit-face. *Time to pop some fucking pimples.* I clench my fists.

He pulls out his nightstick.

"Oh, that's nice. Let's go another round." I spin to the mirror. "Your 'transparency' bullshit? A woman? Fucking assholes!"

Two more guards come to Lowry's side. They give him a signal.

Now it's a fair fight.

Their hands slide behind their backs, and they step aside, showing me the exit.

What the— My rage sputters. I glare at them. They stare straight ahead.

I get in their faces. They don't move. Not a flinch.

A door shuts down the hall. It's silent now.

They're giving up on me.

I see a window. I see the sky and trees. Freedom.

But it's a mirage. Out there is more of the same. *Stuck.* Out there nothing makes a difference.

But in here, one thing does. She's sick. We're running out of time.

13. SUBMISSION

"You want to walk away from this family and everything I created? Chase this dream of becoming a doctor? Then you better be the best. You better become a machine."

Greg appeared lost in thought, regarding his new bionic knee somberly. Frustration quickly set in, as he failed to escape his pillow fortress on the couch.

Kevin wagged a finger from the recliner. *Stay put.*

Jasper entered from the kitchen. Kevin's Christmas card from two years ago caught his gaze. Kevin and Alex, with their arms around a golden retriever in their front yard. He traced the border of Alex's face. He shifted to the beaming blonde woman draped over them.

"Did you meet Susan in the hospital?" Kevin asked.

Jasper shook his head and stepped back. "Sunny winter," he said, pointing at the card. "Ours were too."

"Yeah?" Kevin asked.

"Miami."

"I love it there. Going home for the holidays?"

"Not this year. My mom can't take time off." Jasper sat on a stool and gripped it tightly.

"What about your dad?"

"He's not around anymore." Through the window, an amber leaf hovered behind his shoulders before it spiraled into the pile of lumber. "Dr. Bishop ... I think we need to tell him."

Greg couldn't look away from Jasper's strained face. His swollen postoperative hands fumbled with a pill bottle at his side. He managed to feed himself a Percocet.

Kevin took in the looks between them. "What's wrong?"

Jasper's mouth opened, his eyes still on Greg, before he faced Kevin. "It's about what happened to Alex. He—"

"Stop." Greg seemingly folded in on himself, clenched. "This has to come from me." His sunken eyes slowly climbed to meet his son's. "Something happened in the trauma bay with Alex that we can't ... explain."

Kevin felt pins creep up his neck. "Okay."

"We had to use internal defibrillation, but when I went to shock, my knee gave out and the paddles ... slipped off his heart." His mouth locked. He looked at Jasper.

"The shock fired next to his heart and there was a blue light between the paddles," Jasper said.

"Like a spark or something?" Kevin asked.

Greg regained his composure. "Three arcs of blue light. I saw it when I fell. Jasper said it lasted longer than a spark. Few seconds."

Kevin's eyes darted between them. "The paddles misfire and you think that changed Alex?"

Greg rolled onto his arm to directly address his son. "Have you heard of internal defibrillation paddles misfiring?"

"I'm sure there are faulty ones, right?"

"Not inside the chest. No reports."

It was a few weeks into anatomy lab when Kevin first saw the paddles. They were awkwardly simplistic, almost like extra-large versions of circular dental mouth mirrors. He rotated them in his mind. *The only way they can shock something is if they contact it, so what the hell was between Dad's paddles?* "It lasted longer than a second? You saw it too?"

Jasper nodded.

"Visited Professor Mobley at your alma mater, Kev," Greg said. "He's never heard of anything like this either." He squeezed a pillow. "I prayed at church for the first time since Linda died. This thing, this event ... it has me in its grip. I just can't figure it out. I don't understand it."

The room faded away around Kevin. He was alone on a dock; on a body of water that he'd never seen before. He took a step and a wooden plank snapped under his weight and fell into the water. He looked up, following the decaying wood to its end, and he saw Alex's empty bed from the psych ward. *Dad, what happened to him?*

Kevin felt cold, then an urge to move. To run right out of his own skin. He pulled the lever of the recliner and sat up, closing his eyes. *God, help me. Help my son.*

Prayer.

His eyes opened. He forced himself to breathe. "We've heard crazy stories that we can't explain like people waking up in the morgue. What if this is something similar?"

"Then what do we do?" Greg asked.

Kevin saw his father drowning, out of reach. He dove in.

"Why don't you write a case report?"

Greg snorted.

"You saw something that three doctors in this room can't comprehend," Kevin said.

"And you think adding more confused doctors will help? Thousands more? We'd get laughed at by every journal," Greg said. "Speculation and research are oxymorons."

"What's our play then, Coach?" Kevin glared at him. "While my son sits in his own shit."

Greg shook his head. He looked outside.

"Dr. Bishop, I ..."

Greg swiveled to Jasper.

He held up his hands. "I know this sounds crazy, but I need a senior project anyway. I'd be happy to do the write-up. With your guidance ..."

"This is the start of your career. Do you really want to tarnish it?" Greg's eyes narrowed. "'We saw a light inside my grandson and now he's acting weird.' How do you think that sounds? Show me what textbook chapter that's in."

"This may be the start of a new chapter," Kevin said. "How many innovators were doubted at first?"

"Doubted? How about *vilified*. Remember Semmelweis? One of the pioneers of antiseptic techniques? The establishment destroyed his reputation, and he ended up in a psychiatric asylum."

Kevin stood. "Which is exactly where Alex has been for a week now. He's not eating, he's losing weight fast. We have to do something."

"If this gets us some answers, and we can help him, I'm all in," Jasper said.

"Dad, you're retired. You have nothing to lose and I'm sure the Bishop name still carries some weight." He turned to his Christmas card. "Alex needs us. And you need to tell Susan."

14. Homecoming

Closing early to the public tonight. Bring your new lady for a drink? 11?

"I'm glad you texted, Judy." Kevin placed Grace's purse on a hook under the bar. "I really need this."

"Of course," Judy said. "Sometimes it helps to get out of the house and change things up." She glanced back at the bottles. "The usual?"

He nodded.

"How about her?"

"Same."

"A whiskey girl? I like her already." Judy poured the glasses. "Do you?"

"Yes."

She leaned forward. "Does she get you?"

Kevin felt warmth flow across his shoulders. He nodded.

"You didn't hesitate." She smiled, placing the glasses in front of him, then paused. His forehead was straining to pull his eyelids up. "When was the last time you had a good night's sleep? You're banged up, like the night we met."

"That bad, huh? I can't remember." He stared at a murky bottle on the bottom shelf. *Charred bile.* "I was with my son yesterday. He's wasting away. The only time he'll eat is if Susan begs him to. Can't sustain this."

"I'm sorry, Kevin."

He swallowed.

"It's times like these I turn to faith. Give up control and trust things will work out," Judy quietly offered.

"I hope it does for James too. Radio silence for a month," he said.

"You know how he is. Isolates when he's having a tough time." She shook her head. "You sure you want to drink tonight?"

Kevin sighed. He reached for it and stopped.

"I'll hold onto this one." She slid it back.

Grace returned from the bathroom and settled next to him at the bar. "It's great to finally meet you. Kevin has the nicest things to say."

Judy bowed. "He's one of the good ones. So glad to meet you as well."

"And thanks for the special treatment tonight." Grace took a sip. "Yum."

"Anything for my VIPs. I needed an early night anyway." She leaned on her elbows. "Kevin, I know you liked Luis, but I want you to meet my new bartender. I think I found a good one." She pounded the bar with her fist. "Barkeep! Shots of the good stuff!"

Her office door opened, and James stepped out in a white collared shirt and dress pants.

"What? No way!" Kevin shouted.

Grace ran around the bar to hug him.

"We missed you, man," Kevin said.

"How do you like my new gig? My boss is pretty cool," James said.

Judy ruffled his black hair. She stopped to admire its new length. "I dunno, he may have you beat, Kevin." She winked and disappeared into her office.

"I'll never hear the end of that," Kevin said.

"Sure won't." James reached for the tequila.

Kevin laughed. "Classic."

They drank the shots. Kevin winced and coughed.

James pointed at his twisted face. "Classic." He filled a pitcher of beer. "Back room?"

They passed through the curtain into their shiny new headquarters. There were upgrades all around. A new table, chairs, and the *Women of the Beach* calendar had met its merciful end, replaced by a collage of *Nightcap* photos.

"My first order of duty," James said. He pointed to a photo of him and Kevin in the corner, smiling in their college sweatshirts. "Life sure has kicked our asses since then."

Kevin kissed Grace's hand. "With a few exceptions."

"You're welcome."

James sat and snapped open his Zippo lighter. Snap. Snap. No flame. He flipped it shut. "I was given a bad conduct discharge."

Grace closed her eyes. "James ..."

"Fuck, I'm sorry," Kevin said.

"Me too. Forfeiture of all pay. Lost my Navy benefits. I'm done." James cleared his throat.

With anyone else, Kevin wouldn't have noticed that anxious tic, but for James it was wounded despair. It was defeat.

"Judge said I could be reinstated if I took corrective measures," James said. "Then that smug son of a bitch Kedge came up to me after, made it seem like he was doing me a favor, but I got the last word like I always do, Sticks. Looked him right in the eye and said, 'I'm coming for you.'"

Beer rushed into Kevin's nose mid-gulp. He choked.

"That's one way to handle it," Grace said to James.

"Not my finest moment," James conceded, "but I wanted it to be his last memory of me." His eyes were low, staring into the corner of the small room. He finished his drink and excused himself to the bathroom.

"I've never seen him like this," Grace said.

Kevin was back in the Charity Hospital boardroom with his three medical directors, the firing squad. He could still hear their condescension, their flat tones, coming from their unforgiving faces. Ruthless finality.

"I have to tell him. He feels lost and alone. He has to know I went through this too," Kevin said.

"He's raw. Maybe now's not the best time."

They sat in concerned silence. Kevin refilled James's drink.

James parted the curtain. "I could've put out a fire with that hose."

"Gosh, how're you single?" Grace laughed and shoved him down in his seat. She wrapped her arms around him. "What can we do? What do you need?"

"Just this." James gave her arms a squeeze. "Man, this is brutal, I feel like I've been tarred and feathered."

"Buddy, I ..." Kevin started.

Grace glanced at him.

"I know what you're going through. I didn't tell you the whole story, about what happened at my job."

She returned to her seat.

"You did." James leaned in quizzically. "Here at this table. You were burnt out and bailed." He took another swig.

"I didn't quit. I was fired."

His mug slowly returned to the table. "What?"

"A patient died because of a medication I gave at the wrong time. Then I gave a dangerous amount of medication to a pediatric patient, who thankfully survived. They were accidents, but I didn't document them well in the patients' charts, so the directors couldn't understand my reasoning. The final straw was when I asked another doctor for help with an intubation, and he ruptured my patient's trachea and the blame fell on me. I tried but I couldn't defend myself, and ultimately, I was the new guy. I was expendable."

James was quiet.

"I should've told you the truth. I'm sorry. I was just ... ashamed," Kevin said. "I want you to know that I *know* how cold those bastards at the table can be and you'll bounce back even stronger."

James looked at Grace. "You knew about this?"

She nodded cautiously.

He took a deep breath. "It hurts that you felt you couldn't tell me. I know we were in different cities, but I'd like to think I could've helped you through it."

"I'm sorry," Kevin said.

"Didn't know lying was part of your repertoire." James glared at him, but it softened. "I have to own my side too.

I disappeared and kept you guys in the dark. I'm sorry. It must have worried you."

"Yeah, a little bit!" Grace punched him in the arm. "We love you."

"Thanks for saying that," Kevin said to James.

"You know I always come back," James said. "Can we agree we'll be upfront with each other? Like the old days?"

"Yes," Kevin said. "Remember our code, 911? Whenever you need me, I'll be there. It still stands."

Kevin recalled the first time the number appeared on his pager in high school. He sped to James's house and saw him stumble down the front steps, shirt torn, holding his bleeding ear. His father was yelling inside.

Passenger door was open, ready for him, and it always was. Let's get lost for a while.

"Still stands." James nodded and kicked back in his chair. "How's Alex? I really miss him."

"He hasn't left the psychiatric unit."

"What? No change?"

Kevin shook his head. "He doesn't care about anything or anyone. He can't function."

"Damn. Not Alex. I've seen that in guys with PTSD. Robots."

"A second psychiatrist I talked with agrees it's schizoid personality disorder," Kevin said.

"Not the trauma?" James scoffed. "I don't know, some of these psychiatrists need psychiatrists ..."

"This time they may have gotten it right," Kevin said. *The person I talk with ... The person I come to visit ... The person who won't respond to me*
   ... That's not my son.

Test Subject 1
Interaction 5
Ford Hospital
040900SMAY19

Canceled due to illness

15. ROOM FOR MORE

Soft light from the backyard faintly illuminated the living room. *Not moonlight ... gold. Dad must be out there.*

A yell pierced the silence. Then Kevin heard a thud.

"Dad?!" Kevin shot through the side door and found Greg outside, sitting amidst the lumber. "Are you hurt? Is it your knee?!"

Greg shook his head. "Dropped the hammer," he slurred. "I went with it."

Kevin regarded the new uneven side band of the deck. Next to it was an empty bottle of Macallan. "Do you think you're ready to take this on?"

"I have to finish this." Greg staggered to make it to a knee. He flopped back down.

"Dad." Kevin came closer.

Greg waved him off. "What else am I good for? I told Susan everything, and she just walked away. I wrote up Alex's trauma in a case report, and four journals refused to publish it."

"You did the right thing."

"I've done nothing. While my grandson rots in that godforsaken psych ward for almost two months."

Kevin crouched into his line of sight. "You're doing the best you can."

"The only way we can help Alex is with more information. I see that now. We need to get his story out there to see if there are others who have gone through this too."

"And we'll keep trying."

"I'm just trying to make things right," he muttered.

"You're the strongest man I know, and you've always done it on your own."

"Always had to."

"Not anymore. Please let me in."

Greg leaned back.

"I'm your family. I'm your blood." Kevin stood and held out his hand. "Let me help."

Greg's hard face trembled. A sigh escaped his lips.

"Let me help," Kevin repeated.

His father took one last look at the hammer on the grass, before he sent his arm out and reached for Kevin.

Kevin hoisted him to his feet and slid underneath his arm, steadying him. *It's time.*

They stumbled back to the kitchen, a unit of pain with four legs walking under the force of two wills.

Greg made an unsightly peanut butter sandwich, ate half of it, and passed out in his chair. Kevin slept on the couch.

That morning, Kevin found Greg sleeping at the table, with mail stuck to his face. He gently lifted his head and peeled off a pamphlet from the Journal of United Emergency Physicians.

Greg opened his heavy eyelids.

"Want me to throw this out?" Kevin asked.

He sat up and winced, slowly extending his knee. "Let me see it." *Chris Denali, MD, Editor-in-Chief.* "Holy shit," he exclaimed. "I know him. Chris was my favorite resident of the last ten years. Look at him now."

"Another Bishop protégé success story."

Greg thumbed through the first few pages. He stopped on Denali's photo. "He's an interesting guy. I think his mother was a shaman, or something." He conjured a last stab at hope. "He may be our shot. We should try the article with him."

Kevin went to the refrigerator. He poured a glass of orange juice.

Greg stiffened. "Or do you have a better plan?"

Kevin handed him the juice and a Tylenol. "Time for you to work."

That afternoon, Greg submitted to the tiny journal. He was good at schmoozing editors, boasting twenty-three publications to his credit. But he wasn't good at filling the time that came with waiting for a response, and with every trip to visit Alex, he was reminded just how dangerous waiting was. His grandson's ribs were now visible, his skin was ghostly white.

Several agonizing weeks later, while skimming through old issues of medical journals, Greg received the email. The journal accepted their case report, and it would be published next month.

Yes. Publication twenty-four was the sweetest. *Finally, some fucking progress. Hopefully someone out there can help, Alex, because we don't have any answers.*

He met Jasper and Kevin that night at Luigi's Pizzeria to celebrate. The owners were family friends, and they saved Greg's favorite table. Through the haze of his third beer, he thought he saw Linda, gazing at him above the red and white plaid tablecloth. *It's not the same without you. Nothing is.* A sudden quiet pulled him back into the moment: Kevin and Jasper were having a chugging contest. Kevin won. Greg smiled.

———

That smile was soon buried under the first snowfall of the season.

Their new hope from the publication met the brutal reality of its reception. A litany of critiques, often cruel and unhelpful, invaded Greg's inbox. Jasper's residency transformed into a junior high school; a place where doctors, like children, tested their unfiltered snipes. Jasper felt as though humanity had devolved back to a crude primality. Each moment was an opportunity to inflict wounds to his psyche, self-worth, and credibility.

"Did Dr. Bishop really let you publish that?"

"That must've been stressful. Are you sure the blue light wasn't a hallucination?" This last had been asked with a knowing smirk, as some residents chuckled to each other in the corner.

And then there was Peggy. She never saw the blue light and she resented Greg's favoritism toward Jasper.

She believed their report was fabricated, and she wasn't bashful about sharing her opinion. Doubt turned into distrust. Without Greg there to defend him, Jasper lost standing in the program. His chief duties were reassigned.

Any hope of finding answers about the significance of the blue light appeared to be lost.

"I wish I had known this was happening to you. I can call Delany," Greg said from his rocking chair.

Jasper watched the steam of his breath slowly unfurl in the winter air. He adjusted the collar of his North Face jacket just as a sharp gust hit a pocket of nervous sweat between his skin and collar. He felt cold, and alone.

"Thank you, but please don't. I think I need to focus on my patients."

"You don't deserve any of this."

"Neither do you." Jasper stood up and stamped his frozen feet.

Chirp, chirp. Greg searched the porch for the origin of the sound. Chirp, chirp. He had forgotten it was his new phone alert. He stopped on an email labeled urgent:

Dr. Bishop,

I'm sure you're getting a lot of negative feedback about your article. I applaud your bravery. I need to speak with you. It's of the utmost importance.

Steven Ikahashi, MD

Associate Professor of Trauma Surgery, Emory University
Attending Physician, Valley Green Hospital
(855) 555-0184

Greg dropped the phone in his lap. He rocked, as a montage of recent insults replayed in his mind. *If this bastard rips into us too ...* he shook away the whispers. "Let's go inside."

They took off their jackets and made their way to the dining table. Jasper sat.

"What's going on?"

Greg handed him his phone.

Jasper read the email before returning it to him. He slouched, shrugged.

Greg paced, eyeing the phone as if it was an opposing boxer. *Twelfth and final round. Finish the fight.* He joined Jasper at the table, dialed, and hit speakerphone.

It rang once.

"This is Dr. Ikahashi."

Greg took a moment to register his shrill pitch.

"Hello?"

"This is Dr. Greg Bishop."

"I bet you've had quite the few weeks," Dr. Ikahashi said.

Greg glanced at Jasper. "You have no idea."

"I do, I do. And that's why I need to speak with you. Hmmm, how do I say this, well I'll just be forthright. Your patient is not the only one. There are four others."

16. Expanding the Database

Greg and Jasper stared at each other in disbelief.

"How did you find them?" Jasper blurted.

"Who else is there?" Dr. Ikahashi's voice rose an octave.

Jasper's hand shot to his mouth. "Sorry. I'm Jasper Richardson, one of the co-authors."

"You're a resident, correct?"

Jasper paused, air seemingly leaking out of his chest. "Yes."

"Greg, can I call you Greg? Greg, I'd like to speak with you alone. No residents."

Greg rolled his eyes. "Sure, Steven."

"Kick a guy when he's down," Jasper said under his breath, now appearing fully deflated. He tried to find his feet and stand.

Greg motioned for him to stay. "One moment." He simulated Jasper's departure by closing the closet door in the hallway. "Okay, it's just me."

"Thank you," Steven said. "You've had quite the career, Greg. Impressive list of accolades."

"It's been rewarding. Frustrating end to it, sadly."

"Frustrating start to mine," Steven said. "Sitting on this knowledge for five years."

"Five years?"

"I'm sure we went through similar progressions. Who do I tell? What would it do to my career? The latter was a risk I couldn't take ... not yet."

Greg looked at Jasper. "We didn't have the luxury of waiting. It's personal."

"I don't follow," Steven said.

"The patient was my grandson."

The line went quiet.

"I see. That's unfortunate." Steven's last syllable was particularly sharp, contrasting with another long pause that followed. "Well, in the spirit of collegial discourse, would you like to hear about the others?"

"Please." Greg snapped his fingers and mimed writing. Jasper fetched him a pen and pad.

"Good. I just need a signature from you first. Give me your fax number and let me know when you receive it."

Greg's fax machine awoke minutes later and spit out a solitary piece of paper. It was a non-disclosure agreement.

Jasper came around the table and peered over Greg's shoulder.

"Received it," Greg said, rubbing his brow.

"It's a bilateral agreement, of course. We hope to learn from you as well."

"We?" Greg asked.

"You'll notice two signatures below mine. They're physicians that work with me. One of them is also my legal counsel and he drafted the agreement," Steven said.

"Is all this really necessary?" Greg asked.

"I won't proceed until it's signed and returned."

Greg hit mute. He scanned the document. Steven Ikahashi, MD, Inc ... Trade secrets involving the acquisition and significance of the blue light seen during thoracotomy ... Confidentiality is for an indefinite period ...

"He knows how to find the blue light," Greg said.

Jasper shifted in his seat. "Should we talk to a lawyer?" he asked.

Greg thought of Alex's frail frame, ravaged by months of inactivity. *We can't wait any longer. What other option do we have anyway?* He signed and faxed it back. Unmuted.

"Good," Steven said. "Let me start by saying all four were my patients, all had penetrating trauma to the chest, all received thoracotomies, all required shocks for arrhythmias and were highly unlikely to survive. Each time there were three seconds of blue light during internal defibrillation, much like you witnessed."

Jesus. Greg scribbled.

"Reading your case report brought back memories of the first encounter. Thirty-one-year-old female, stabbed in the chest. I was bumped by a nurse when I deployed the shock. Thirty joules of energy, same as you. She woke up emotionless, much like your patien ... grandson. She was quite colorful before."

"Definitely a parallel there. Did psychiatry admit her?"

"No. Her impairment wasn't severe, but the family was quite upset. No word from them since. The second was a fifty-year-old male stabbed in the chest. Time of death was called, but he still had some cardiac activity. After people left the room, I went back in with the defibrillator and found the blue light."

Greg's pen stopped. He flashed to Alex with Jasper back in the trauma bay learning how to intubate the old man who had just died. This felt different.

"That's a slippery slope," he said.

"An invaluable one," Steven said defensively. "I discovered I could reliably find the blue light. His wife told me he wanted to donate his body to science. I just expedited the process."

Greg slowly exhaled. He looked at the pad. After the last word his hand was looping a small, black circle.

"Shall I continue?"

Down the rabbit hole we go. "Yes."

"Sixty-seven-year-old woman shot in the chest. Against all odds, she survived. That time I had used fifty joules, to see if higher energy would make a difference. She became kind, patient, and thoughtful. She was previously known to be hostile and reclusive. It took us four phone calls to find anyone willing to even talk about her.

"The last case was an eleven-year-old male shot in the chest. Drive-by shooting, and he was collateral damage. He was another one I thought didn't have a chance. Ten joules of energy. The blue light was smaller, more proportional to his size. When he woke up, he was different too. He was manipulative. Wicked. His Boy Scout troop came to the hospital. Know the case?"

Greg collapsed back in his chair. "Yes." It was a year ago, front page of the health section. *Boy Scout Tragedy.* The patient was shot dead in the hospital in front of the whole troop after he tried to grab a security officer's gun. You don't forget stories like that.

"And it gets even more peculiar," Steven said. "Remember the second patient who wanted to donate his body to science? He became a cadaver at our medical school. I found him, but no blue light. It was gone. There were twenty cadavers in that lab with open chests. Not a single one had the blue light."

Greg shook his head. *Well, at least there's finally one thing that's consistent.* Outside, he saw a squirrel jump into his satellite dish. He traced the cord back to the receiver. "Do you think the defibrillators played a role? Did you use a different one in the cadaver lab?"

"Same model, and it was biphasic every time. You?"

"Biphasic. I wonder what would happen if you used monophasic? Different current vector?" Greg's curiosity was piqued.

"Intriguing, yes. Dr. Bishop. Come visit me in Atlanta. I'm sure the local gun and knife club will bring us plenty of business."

Greg ran his thumb over the engraving of his pocket watch.

"I think we could help each other," Steven continued. "Your name brings credibility and I have friends who could be very interested in supporting us."

Greg looked at Jasper. "I'll consider it under one condition. I get to bring my team."

Jasper blushed.

"One's the resident you kicked off the line. He was in the trauma bay when it happened."

Steven let out a breath laced with irritation. "Understandable. He wrote the article with you. Have him sign the form and refax it."

"The other is my son, who's an emergency physician as well. He's the father of the patient."

A chilly silence emanated from the phone. Then the words, "Absolutely not."

"Why? I'm the grandfather, we already crossed that line," Greg said.

"You and the resident were inside the chest. You've seen what we've seen. No skeptics, no family feuds. We need to maintain some objectivity here."

Greg stifled an outburst. *Nothing about this is objective*! *What facts do we even have?* He stewed in silence. *Make that bastard wait.*

Jasper reached for the pen and pad. He wrote and flipped it for Greg to read:

He's holding the cards

Greg closed his eyes. He saw Kevin above him in the backyard, arm extended. *How could I possibly leave you in the dark?* He curled forward onto his elbows, nauseous. "So how do you make sense of all this?"

"I'm sure you've exhausted thinking about it from a scientific perspective. I know I have." Steven was calm now. "Take a step back. We're dealing with a novel entity, manipulated by energy, possibly pure energy itself, that governs the essence of who we are. It disappears when we die."

The air froze in front of Greg. He felt it inside his chest for the first time, in all its majesty. A wave of excitement washed over him, but as it receded in the riptide, he felt pure terror. "The soul."

"Precisely."

Test Subject 2
Interaction 7
Ford Hospital
041300SMAY19

Informed Consent for Pneuma Transplant

<u>Today we will be assessing whether you:</u>
[X] Understand the transplant process including the procedural details, risks, benefits, and alternatives
[] Express a choice on whether to proceed consistent with your preferences and values
[] Appreciate the consequences of participating or refusing
[] Show appropriate reasoning when comparing these consequences

[X]: Denotes the objective has been completed
[]: Denotes the objective is still pending

This interaction is being video recorded.

———

"This procedure may not work, and it may kill you," my interviewer says.

"If it doesn't work, I'll kill myself anyway."

He comes to a standstill. *Oh yes, that made him uncomfortable.* He wants to look at the mirror, but he doesn't.

"You're in all black today, ready for the cemetery," I say. "Maybe you can be a part of my funeral procession."

He closes a folder and puts it under the table. *No doubt buying time to find the right words.*

"Have you thought about suicide a lot?"

I nod.

"Do you have a plan?" he asks.

"Jump off an overpass into traffic."

"You'd definitely make local news."

"Do you think I give a shit about stardom?"

He shakes his head.

"It'd be my last chance to rattle some cages."

"And you'd likely kill people. You don't have any notches on that belt yet."

"I'm warming to the idea. Can you imagine? So much blood and metal."

"Sadly, I can." He regards the barren room. "Dying on the table wouldn't be the grand exit you described, but unfortunate, nonetheless. While I personally think you'll survive it, the other subject won't."

My eyes shoot to him. *Since when was that part of the deal?* Something inside me shakes. "Can't save her, huh? And I know she's a woman, let's cut the crap."

"She opted not to. How does that make you feel?"

She's sacrificing herself ... for me.

I look around. It's nighttime in my childhood home. I can see light underneath a door. There's warmth. I reach for it and turn the knob. Locked. I step back into the cold, dark hallway.

"If she wants to be a martyr, then so be it," I say.

"Nothing else?"

"What more is there? She signed her life away. Game over."

"Okay." He raps his knuckles on the table. "Want to end early?"

There's twenty minutes left in the session. "What, now?"

"Yes."

"Whatever." I reach for my jacket and a whiff of perfume stops me cold.

Mom ...

My breathing quickens. I try to steady myself, but I can only groan and fold my arms. *Mom.*

She's with Dad in the teacup at Disneyworld. I've never seen her so happy.

A feeling I don't recognize spreads through me. *I miss them.* The tears come. "What are you doing? Are you messing with me?!"

He reaches underneath and pulls out the folder. "That was for us. We needed to see something worth fighting for."

17. Stretch

Six night shifts in a row. Kevin's sixth ended with a woman sobbing while he repaired the laceration on her hand. "I walked into our house, and they were doing it on my couch! And she was wearing my feather boa! He didn't mean to throw the chair at me. I think he was scared I would leave. Oh, please hurry, I need to get home to my husband!"

Kevin normally would have been concerned about this woman's spiral, but today, his empathy tank was empty. Too many days without sleep; too much pain in his inner circle. "I'm done." Kevin bandaged her wound. "We'll see you back here in ten days and we'll take the sutures out."

I'm done.

He stared at a concrete wall, waiting for his car and heart to warm. *Make it all stop.* No talking, no texting. He turned his phone off, pulled out of the parking lot and reached a red light. An elderly woman was trying to cross the street. She was only halfway when the light turned green then red again. He rolled down the window. "Are you serious? Get ..." He forced his jaw shut, his anger shifting to an inflatable snowman waving at him from the sidewalk. *Merry Christmas.*

He made it to his father's driveway as the first rays of sun danced across his neck. He turned off the car and rested his head on the steering wheel. *I can't go in there.* His eyes landed on his crumpled workout clothes. *Fuck it. Run.*

Kevin chased the sunlight through the buildings, out of shape, and out of his mind. He left the pavement and broke into a sprint, pounding up the hill. *Feel the pain. Find her tree.* He saw the oak's barren branches come into view, then, by its trunk, he saw Susan.

His sneakers skidded to a stop on the dead grass.

She regarded him with a soft smile that quickly left.

Kevin walked toward her. She'd lost at least twenty pounds. *She can't handle this stress much longer.*

"I had to get out of there, and I had nowhere to go," she said.

"Is your hotel okay? Are you getting any sleep?"

"Yes. No." Susan took a deep breath. "You've always seemed happier when you've visited here, so I thought I'd give it a shot."

Kevin nodded.

"I found her initials." Her eyes climbed the tree to its towering limbs. "I've never seen the tree in the winter. It's kind of scary, actually."

He followed her gaze. "Crazy how something so majestic could change into something that looks so dark and twisted."

Susan looked out to the horizon. She reached into her bag and pulled out a cigarette.

"Haven't seen that since college," Kevin said.

She lit it and took a drag, squinting at him. "You know how Alex is. I could never get away with this at home. Now ..." She shrugged. "Just please don't lecture me, doc."

Kevin bit his lip. He folded his hands and took in the view.

"You haven't come to see us this week," she said.

"Getting killed at work. Finally have a break."

She lowered herself onto a root. "I know I'm not easy ... and I know you're not in love with me anymore. Haven't been for a while."

He opened his mouth to speak.

"I understand. We'll be okay." Her voice faltered, tears welling in her eyes. "But our boy's getting worse. He's not eating at all, and the doctors are pushing for a feeding tube. I need you to do something. Anything."

"I ..." Words crawled up the back of Kevin's tongue before retreating into darkness. "We published the case report, Susan. His story is out there now."

"Right, Greg's article. The world knows our tragedy." She took another drag and looked at him through the smoke. "And?"

"They've heard some responses but-"

"They?"

"Dad and Jasper, the resident I told you about."

She waited. "And?"

"They haven't said much this week." He paused.

She cocked her head.

"Other than Dad's going to Atlanta today," he said.

She ashed the cigarette before shifting to pick at her fingers. "Why, Kevin?"

Stop picking your fingers! You'll have nothing left. He tried to steady his reeling mind. "I think they're meeting with someone who read the article. Dad didn't go into details, but he would tell me if it was something big."

He didn't believe the words the minute they left his mouth.

She saw his dismay and pressed forward. "Your father, Dr. Skeptical, who's left Illinois maybe twice in his life, is getting on a plane today? And it has to do with our son?"

Kevin sank. *He shut me out.* "What can I—"

"Get on that plane." Susan stood. "You can't let them do this on their own. There's too much at stake. Do you hear me?" She flushed. "This is *our boy* and he's dying."

Kevin's worst fear churned with unbearable force. *I may lose Alex forever. He's nineteen and about to get a feeding tube? I have to do more!* He looked at her, his nerves firing frenetically. "I'll fix this."

She placed her hands on his shoulders. "Promise?"

He stayed on her face. "Yes."

She embraced him and quickly slid off. As Susan walked away, she eyed the tree one last time. "You're right, there's something about this place." Her footsteps faded down the hill.

Kevin unclenched his freezing hands, alone, at the summit. He turned on his phone. Texts and a missed call from Grace.

He texted her:

I have to go to Atlanta today. It's about Alex. I'll explain everything when I get back. I love you

He stood in the silhouette of the oak. There were days when the magic happened. Time slowed, and things felt lighter. Days when he felt a deep assurance. Today wasn't one of them. Today, it was just a bare tree.

18. Southern Charm

Greg carefully led Jasper down the aisle of their plane at O'Hare Airport. They found their seats in row twenty-seven in the back, where Greg informed Jasper it was safest. Jasper begrudgingly wedged himself into the middle seat, pinned between Greg's shoulder and his equally massive neighbor. He felt their size spill over their seats and pour out on him. He soon resigned himself to his lot for the next few hours and allowed himself to nestle into the abundant flesh blanketing his sides. He shut his eyes and rested.

Ten minutes passed. Greg heard the clink of bottles behind him. He watched the flight team load whiskey in the galley, the antidote for his mounting aerophobia. He tried to distract himself with the aircraft safety card. Someone stopped next to him in the aisle.

"Dad."

Greg flinched. He slowly looked up.

"Next time you sign a non-disclosure agreement, make sure the conversation isn't recorded." Kevin glared, his phone near Greg's face.

Greg froze on the screen. There he was with Jasper at the dining table speaking to Steven on the phone. *I never took the security cameras down.*

"Let's talk more when we land."

Kevin put on his headphones and returned to his seat, four aisles up.

"Fuck," Jasper whispered.

Greg slid the card into the seatback in front of him. He lowered his head. Then he smiled.

———

They landed in Atlanta where a cold snap was beginning to mellow. Kevin looked out and caught the fading winter sun reflected on the wing. He steeled himself for the battle ahead and joined the exiting throng.

Two hours later, as the trio peeled off their layers and entered the lobby of Valley Green Hospital, a thin man in business casual descended upon them. He stopped shy of hand-shaking distance, pausing on each of them through his thin-rimmed glasses.

"There are three of you."

Kevin recognized his voice from the video and extended his hand. "I'm Kevin Bishop, nice to—"

Doctor Ikahashi turned abruptly to Greg. "Isn't this the man I explicitly said was not to come here?"

Kevin returned his arm to his side.

"He knows nothing," Greg said. "He found my boarding pass and got on our flight."

Steven stared past them, shaking his head. He pulled out his phone and sent a text. His black crew cut rotated back. "Come with me."

They walked down a green tiled corridor and stopped outside a conference room. "Wait here," Steven said and closed the faux-wooden door behind him.

After around thirty minutes, the door opened and an enormous man with emerald eyes stepped out. He regarded Greg with a flash of intrigue at seeing a fellow mountain. "I'm Aaron Coates. I'm a psychiatrist here and legal counsel for Dr. Ikahashi."

He shook Kevin's hand last and held it. Kevin matched his grip.

Aaron stepped back, studying him. "Whatever you claim to know or not know is inconsequential. Your father and Dr. Richardson have signed non-disclosure agreements and your presence here could easily be inferred as a violation. We've decided not to continue with you and ask—"

"May I have a word?" Kevin gestured down the hall.

Aaron's muscular chest swelled, testing the strength of the threads on his shirt buttons. "There's nothing left to—"

Kevin started walking. He approached a small table in the empty cafeteria, sat, and looked back.

Aaron, mouth stuck mid-sentence, sought an explanation from Greg and Jasper. They avoided eye contact.

Aaron sighed, then followed. He lowered himself onto a plastic chair. It screamed under his weight.

Kevin's eyes skated past a Christmas tree in the corner, and then settled on Aaron's wedding ring. "Have any kids?"

"You called me over here just to ask me that?"

Kevin nodded. He noticed another ring: a diamond-studded football. "Any boys?"

Aaron withdrew his hands from the table. "Two."

"Well, I only have Alex. He's my everything."

He glanced at Kevin's bare ring finger.

"Sophomore at UCLA, state champion swimmer in high school, such a promising future, gone. You read what happened to him, but you don't know the latest. He's been in a psych ward for months. Medications. Electroconvulsive therapy. Nothing works, and he's given up. He's sickly thin. It's worse than you can imagine, and it's burying us alongside him."

His eyes fell. "You have my sympathies."

"I know that scripted response. It's for your patients. I need much more than that. I need you to *feel it*, as a father."

Aaron returned to his face.

There was a glimmer of hope. Kevin took a deep breath. "Alex needs us. I can give you access to speak with him whenever you want, and I could give you a full profile of what he was like before."

Aaron's arms folded. "You've already breached our trust."

"You can trust them. My father hasn't said anything to me, and you need him. He's one of the biggest names in emergency medicine, not to mention his connections for future publications."

"We are aware. How do we know he hasn't said anything to you?"

Kevin realized there was no way around. No way over. "He didn't need to." He pulled out his phone and hit play.

Aaron's wide eyes watched the security camera video. "Recording a conversation without consent? That's against the law. You somehow think this makes me trust you more?"

"Trust I'll do whatever it takes to get answers for my son. Someone with my motivation could be an asset."

Aaron nodded at a security guard walking by. "And if our answer remains no?"

"Then I'll find another team. People who'd appreciate this video, especially the parts about you manipulating patients without a clue of what you're doing. I'd have to cast a wide net, but thankfully Alex's mom is a publicist."

Aaron stiffened. "This conversation's over." He stood.

Kevin held the line. "I'll be here."

Back in the hallway, Greg and Jasper blinked as Aaron barreled down on them.

"Let me get that for you." Jasper reached for the door.

Aaron beat him to it and disappeared into the conference room.

They shared a look and approached Kevin. "Want to share with the class?" Greg asked.

Kevin tapped his phone.

"You didn't," Greg said.

"Fuck," Jasper whispered.

"Since when was that part of the plan?" Greg exclaimed. He sat on the same exhausted plastic chair.

"Wasn't my first choice, but here we are. Strap in."

"Blackmail? This is over. They're probably calling security. We should leave," Greg said. "How far we've come. I can't believe you gambled like that!"

Kevin's eyes stayed low. He let the tirade fade into white noise.

"What do we do now? Jasper, you're the only one at a trauma center. Maybe you—"

They heard the door open. Heavy footsteps. *Aaron.*

None of them dared to move. They braced for impact.

A paper landed in front of Kevin, then a pen.

"We've decided to continue with the three of you. There can be no further misunderstandings."

The Chicago contingent traded surprised looks and quickly hid them. They nodded.

"This is a unique circumstance where family is directly involved. There is nothing clean about this. It is essential for us to be transparent and trust one another," Aaron said.

Kevin perused the non-disclosure agreement. His pen stopped on the signature line.

He was pulled back to the corner of the room. Susan was at the base of the Christmas tree, helping Alex open a present. Grace was at another table, her gaze fixed on Kevin.

He exhaled. His pen didn't move.

"If you need more time I under—"

Kevin signed and handed it back to him. He deleted the video.

Aaron leaned in. "Now delete it again from the recently deleted folder."

He acquiesced.

"Welcome to Valley Green."

They followed Aaron into the conference room and Dr. Clarissa Smith, an emergency physician at the hospital, came around the large rectangular table to greet them.

Steven remained seated at the head. Motionless, he waited for everyone to take their seats, then signaled Aaron.

"We're western physicians. We've been trained, and view the body in very similar ways," Aaron said. "But this is something entirely different. All I ask is that you keep an open mind." He pulled out a notepad from his briefcase. "I'd like to start by summarizing what we have so far, so everyone is on the same page. There are four people in this room who have seen the blue light, and I'm not one of them. Dr. Bishop is the other."

Kevin nodded.

"After extensive review, there are no documented reports outside of what's been seen by people in this room. Do you agree, Dr. Bishop?" Aaron asked.

"Yes. Call me Greg."

Aaron smiled. "Is everyone okay with first name basis?"

They nodded.

"Three seconds of blue light have been seen during biphasic defibrillation in five patients. One patient received ten joules, three received thirty joules, and one received fifty joules. Each produced a different outcome; however, the two surviving patients that received thirty joules had similar outcomes. Now." Aaron rubbed his huge palms together. "Our leading theory of what the blue light represents, however fantastical it may sound, is, for lack of more precise terminology, what we will call the 'soul.' According to the *Oxford English Dictionary*, the soul is defined as 'the spiritual or immaterial part of a human being or animal, regarded as immortal.' What we have discovered challenges this concept. The 'soul' may be a physical object, and whether it is immortal remains to be seen. We are on the verge of creating a new definition of the 'soul,' and we're gaining more insight into its function as well. It appears to be associated with personality. All of these patients underwent drastic personality changes."

"If we are sticking to the *OED* ..." Steven pulled out his phone and read another definition. "By personality we mean 'the combination of characteristics or qualities that form an individual's distinctive character.' Take for instance, our third patient, who was previously unsociable, without a trace of empathy, became compassionate and engaging. Our most recent patient, a happy, loving child, became cruel and dangerous. Even their values changed."

"Yes. And one key issue that we face currently is that there's no academic agreement on the locus of personality or how best to treat personality disorders. Psychotropic medications are rarely effective," Aaron said.

Greg nodded slowly. "They're mostly treated with cognitive behavioral therapy."

"Which is essentially mental reconditioning, right?" Aaron smiled. "Not very effective because we've been searching in the wrong place. The soul's not inside your skull, it's inside your chest, close to your heart."

Kevin flashed to his training in medical school. He recalled from the back row of his psychopathology class. Depression, hallucinations were related to neurotransmitters in the brain. Fear responses were associated with the amygdala. Personality was almost woven into the fabric of who a person was.

An echo sounded in his mind. It was his own voice.

That's not my son.

Aaron just snapped the puzzle piece into place. *This is real and this is really happening. My son's soul is at stake.*

"It's also worth noting," Clarissa said, "that both the soul, and personality, have varied philosophical and theological depictions. It would be short-sighted of us to only consider the western scientific view here. Existentialists believe personality stems from one's conscious experiences, Postmodernists view personality as a function of relations to institutional roles and settings, and religions interpret the concepts very differently. I'm a Christian, and we view elements of personality like emotions, willpower, and moral awareness as synonymous with one's 'heart.' I was pleasantly surprised to find out that's not far from the truth."

"Thank you for bringing that up," Aaron said. "The scope of this is staggering. We need to treat it with the utmost care."

"And closed lips outside of this room," Steven said.

There was a knock at the door. "Dr. Ikahashi?" A nurse informed Steven there was an incoming trauma ten minutes away. Thirty-five-year-old male with multiple gunshot wounds.

"Aaron and Kevin, any interest in seeing what we've seen? Let's catch you up to speed." Steven stood.

Kevin balked. "Now?"

"You traveled all the way here. Were you expecting just a PowerPoint today?" He grinned. "We'll finish our discussion after."

The room was full of people with excited smiles. They stood and headed for the door.

Kevin was slow to rise.

"You okay?" Greg asked under his breath.

"I don't know if I'm ready for this."

"Unexpected, but I think it's important you see it."

"We don't know what we're doing," Kevin said. "We're going to manipulate a patient now? Has Steven gone through a review board? Have you?"

"He said he'll talk about that today. Kevin." Greg held his arm. "We don't have much time. Remember why we're here. This is family."

Which is why it's our duty to do it the right way. He glanced at Steven who was waiting for them by the door.

"What do you think of our little hospital?" Steven asked.

Kevin walked past him. "It's great."

They reached the trauma bay on the heels of the paramedics wheeling a bullet-riddled patient. His shouts devolved into fading whimpers, then silence. The Valley Green team couldn't find a pulse, and within a minute they performed a thoracotomy exposing his mangled lung. His pulse returned after receiving blood and he was quickly transferred to the OR, but the resuscitation fell short.

The trauma surgeon stepped back and introduced Steven and the rest, "Okay everyone, the research team needs the room for a bit. Leave everything and we'll clean up in ten." He departed into the hallway and Steven followed.

The surgical tech and nurse hesitated.

"Just a few measurements. We won't touch anything. All your counts will be correct," Clarissa reassured them.

She waited for the doors to close, confirmed the drained heart was barely beating, and went to work assembling the defibrillator.

Steven soon rejoined them. "I spoke with the family. His body has been donated to science. Let's proceed."

Kevin stared in disbelief. *That's it? That's all they get?* He leaned towards Greg.

Greg waved him off.

"Biphasic first." Steven grabbed the paddles. "Can everyone see? The key is to align your hands like this, near the apex of the heart." He positioned the paddles four centimeters apart, parallel to one another. "Everyone clear?" He deployed the shock.

Kevin gasped. Three arcs of blue lightning flowed between the paddles. Dense with meaning and significance, it was somehow both familiar and alien, and it was the most beautiful thing he'd ever seen.

"Whoa." Aaron laughed nervously. "That was worth the wait."

"Amazes me every time," Steven said.

"Let's try monophasic." Clarissa pulled a second defibrillator out of her duffel bag.

"All clear?" Shock.

The same blue light returned, but something was different. "That's weird, almost like it was vibrating," Jasper said.

"Do it again," Greg said.

Steven deployed another shock and his hand slipped. The blue light moved briefly, mirroring the position of the paddles.

"Whoa. That's new!" Steven said. He verified that everyone saw it.

"The heart stopped," Kevin said.

He attempted one last shock, but the blue light was gone. He granted himself a second of reflection before saying, "Time to pack up."

As they left for the door, Clarissa stayed. "Give me just a moment."

Kevin watched her hold the patient's wrist gently, as she closed her eyes and lowered her head. "Please go with God now," she whispered. "May your transition be smooth and peaceful."

Kevin couldn't help but wonder if she had always prayed when her patients died, or just now out of guilt because *we just moved the very thing you're speaking to.*

Back in the war room, Kevin traced the grooves of the wooden table with his fingers. He stole a look at Clarissa who was visibly shaken.

Steven watched them.

"I'd like to thank our Chicago team, again, for coming out here. I hope everyone shares our excitement." He stood. "For a moment I'd like to discuss the Institutional Review Board. Our investigation falls under *surgical innovation* during an emergency situation, so we don't need to proceed through the IRB."

"It would also take months," Greg added.

Kevin sat up. "Yes, we're dealing with emergency situations, but what we're doing to the patient isn't an emergency intervention. We're talking about changing people's 'souls' here and 'donating their bodies to science' isn't exactly informed consent. Families need to know that their loved ones may survive and be completely different when they wake up. Forever."

Steven sat. "That's the point, they can be changed for the better, but the more information we provide to people outside this room, the more control we lose. And would a family provide consent if they knew what we know?"

"They deserve to know what's at stake," Kevin said.

Steven's hand swept over his lip.

"I think we need a better grasp on this before we dive further into human subjects," Kevin urged.

Greg turned to him. "That's why we're meeting here, to have discussions. What are you suggesting?"

"Today wasn't just a discussion. When you think about the early stages of a scientific experiment, what comes to mind?" Kevin asked.

He was met with blank stares.

"Four legs."

"You can't be serious," Greg said.

"A pig's chest is very similar to a human's, and you've only dealt with patients who were dying," Kevin said. "Plus, it might be interesting to see if they have 'souls' in their own right."

"Where exactly are we going to get pigs?" Clarissa asked.

"I know a guy," Kevin said. "Dad, you have a big backyard."

Greg held up his hands. "This is getting ridiculous. How do you plan to assess a pig's personality?"

"Just because we can't talk to them doesn't mean the experience won't add value. It will help us catch up to Steven in terms of locating the 'soul,' and we can explore this new finding with the monophasic setting."

"You mean the setting where we just moved a man's soul inside his body?" Clarissa challenged. "Didn't that border on desecration?"

"And how was that different from what you've already done?" Kevin asked.

"We've changed it, but we've kept it where it's supposed to be, so maybe that means it can live on in the afterlife. But if we move it, I can't reason that through," she said.

Steven took in their impassioned exchange. He sent a text and nodded at Aaron who passed a form to Greg. "I'm glad we're having these conversations. Brings new perspectives. Kevin, I actually think you should explore this idea," he said. "Let's go down this road together. Do we have a partnership?"

Kevin settled. He nodded.

Greg nodded too. He leaned towards Kevin and whispered, "We need to talk."

"Fantastic." Steven watched them sign more legal forms. "We look forward to meeting Alex." He rose and walked to the door. "The word 'soul' may be triggering for patients and their families. We should consider using a different word, 'pneuma.' Etymologically, it means 'that which is breathed or blown,' but it is also depicted as one's vital spirit. It's Greek like our beloved Hippocrates."

"I like it," Jasper said. "Plus, it's similar to 'pneumo,' or the lungs, which is where it's located."

"Nice," Kevin said.

The room nodded in agreement.

"In that aim, before we wrap up," Steven said, "one of my former patients is here, and she's agreed to answer questions regarding her experience."

Steven looked out the glass windows of the conference room towards a frail, well-dressed woman and signaled her. She opened the door and entered, pulling an oxygen tank. Kevin's focus was drawn to her disarming smile, accentuated by bright peach lipstick. "I'd like you to meet Ms. Katherine Trudy."

Test Subject 1
Interaction 6
Ford Hospital
050900SMAY19

Informed Consent for Pneuma Transplant

<u>Today we will be assessing whether you:</u>
[X] Understand the transplant process including the procedural details, risks, benefits, and alternatives
[X] Express a choice on whether to proceed consistent with your preferences and values
[] Appreciate the consequences of participating or refusing
[] Show appropriate reasoning when comparing these consequences

[X]: Denotes the objective has been completed
[]: Denotes the objective is still pending

This interaction is being video recorded.

———

The albuterol gives me the spins again. *Then again, it could be his big brown eyes.*

The hum of the nebulizer finally stops. Travis listens to my lungs and smiles. "You're improving."

I tap my facemask.

"Need a break?"

"Just from the medicine." My muffled voice leaks out.

He chuckles and slides it off. "I'll reload and be back soon."

He leaves, but not before I catch a glance at his tight trousers. *I'm incorrigible.* My eyes fall to the radio on the nightstand. *That was so sweet of them to get one for me!*

Mr. Montoya enters and flips it on. *Reading my mind, as always.* Beautiful classical music wafts between us. I lean back and enjoy the tranquility before my painful cough ruins the moment.

"I'm sorry," I pant, "I should've asked for help sooner. It escalated so quickly."

"We're just glad you're on the mend." He reaches into a bag. "As you know our care is limited here, so if things worsen, please allow us to take you to the hospital."

"I don't want to be a burden."

"I know."

He places a black box on the bedside tray. "For you. You inspire me."

I open it. A beautiful gold and black chessboard. *It's stunning!* I gaze at him fondly.

"I doubt I'll be anywhere as good as Beatrice," he says.

"I would always beat her anyway."

We share a laugh.

"And out of respect to your wishes, I still haven't contacted her." Mr. Montoya reaches for the box.

I grab it first. "Where do you think you're going with my gift?"

"I thought we could save it for later when you're feeling better?"

"You can't tease me like that," I say coyly. "This'll be my physical therapy for the day." I grab the closest piece. *The rooks have so much detail!*

He takes off his jacket. "Try to be gentle."

I set up the board. She always chose black.

The last time I was with her ... I told her I was moving, and I wouldn't see her again. Nine words were all I could muster. She leaned forward and her glasses fell around her neck. She really saw me. She held my hand softly. "Wherever you're going will be a better place because you're in it. Thank you for being a great friend." She slid her glasses to the bridge of her nose with her pinky. We finished our game in under an hour. I let her win.

I kiss two fingers and touch the corner of the chessboard. *Thank you for being the only one I've ever felt at peace with.*

"Pregame ritual?" he asks.

"Just saying goodbye."

I move my pawn two spaces.

Within minutes he slides his first pawn off the board; he stays on it. "What do you think happens after we die?"

"Shouldn't I ask you that question?"

He brings out his knight. "Our endeavors are limited to the living."

"I'd like to think it's when you sleep but aren't dreaming."

"No afterlife?"

"Dear, if there is one, then things will surely be interesting for me soon."

19. OUTSIDE

"If you need anything, I'll be out front in the truck. I can increase the sedation as needed. After ten minutes you'll probably need another dose of ketamine."

Kevin watched as his father shook the supplier's hand and led him out of the backyard, closing the side gate behind him. He slid a cinder block at the base and lowered his beanie over his ears.

Thank God there's no snow. Dad's irritated enough already.

Kevin joined his father carrying two thoracotomy trays. He shivered. "I think we have everything. We're good."

"Nothing about this is good. You own this," Greg said.

He shivered again.

Jasper was waiting for them at the juncture of brown grass and a big blue tarp, where a row of four pigs lay motionless. "Do I even want to know where they came from?"

"It's one of those 'don't ask, don't tell' things." Kevin handed Jasper a tray and put on his facemask.

They were prepping for surgery in their home.

Armed with protective equipment over their scrubs, and thermal underwear, Greg plugged the defibrillators into the extension cord and checked the power. "Okay let's do a quick recap. The blue light is the soul."

"Pneuma," Jasper said. "We should get used to calling it that, so we don't slip in front of patients."

"Whatever." Greg shot him a look. "Fine. The *pneuma* is electrical energy, so the only way to see and manipulate it is with electrical paddles. There are two defibrillator settings, biphasic and monophasic. So far, shocking the pneuma with biphasic energy can lead to personality change. This is likely what happened to Alex, and our goal has been to figure out how many joules of biphasic energy it will take to change him back to his previous self. It's currently unclear what the monophasic setting does, but it causes the pneuma to vibrate and possibly move, which is why we're experimenting on pigs today. Anything to add?"

"Since we think monophasic energy can move it, we're also interested to see if this setting with a sustained current will give us more time to move it further," Kevin said.

"Yes. Sustained shock means more heat production, so we need to add extra layers, so we don't get burned." Greg said, as they donned thick ski gloves. "Okay, I'll see if I can find the blue light first with the regular monophasic setting, then we can try the sustained monophasic shock. Manufacturer says we can get a max of thirty seconds of monophasic at fifty joules."

He watched Jasper scrub iodine on the marked chest.

"Ready?"

Greg turned on a video camera. All systems go.

Jasper nodded. He made his incision; fat splayed from the wound. He entered Pig One's chest and cranked the rib spreaders.

The hog squealed and convulsed.

Kevin lurched forward. "Dad, should we up the sedation?!"

"He said they may move a little." Greg peered over the fence into the neighbor's yard. "Keep going."

Jasper grunted against one last turn of the handle. Its legs clenched, then relaxed.

Kevin lowered himself to within inches of the gaping, bloody hole. *It's eerily human inside. Remember why you're here. This is for Alex.*

Greg crept forward with the paddles. "Smaller space." He copied Steven's placement. "Like this, right?"

"Yes," Jasper said.

"Clear?" He deployed the shock.

Nothing.

Greg rechecked the defibrillator. The settings were correct.

"It's all about location and hand placement. It was smaller in the pediatric patient in Atlanta. Bring your hands together a centimeter," Jasper said.

"Clear?" Shock.

Three arcs of blurry blue light rippled between the paddles for three seconds.

"Yes!" Jasper pumped his fist. "So cool. I bet all animals have 'souls.' Think about what that—"

"Don't get any ideas, Doolittle. Let's keep moving." Greg switched to the sustained monophasic setting. "Clear?"

"Clear," Jasper muttered.

Shock.

The hazy blue lightning returned. Three seconds passed, but it was still there. Greg rotated his wrists and the captured light moved with him. "Wow. I want to see it up close."

He pulled his hands towards him, lifting it out of the chest. Three beautiful blue waves undulated a foot away from his face.

Jasper glanced at his watch. "Ten seconds."

Things had moved so quickly in Atlanta that Kevin couldn't process them. But now, immersed in the glow of the blue light, something overtook him. The light stained his father's face, deepening his dark lines. He stopped on the innocent pig below them. *This was Alex's chest.*

Kevin's gut split.

The light suddenly disappeared. Greg lowered the paddles. "What happened? We had five more seconds. Did we lose power?!"

Jasper flashed to the machine. "Power's on."

"Did the manufacturer lie to me?"

"Shit, the heart stopped," Jasper said.

Kevin's hands dove inside the chest; he started compressions.

"What're you doing? We have three more pigs," Greg said.

"Do you think he has epinephrine in his truck? Shock the heart! At least give it a chance."

Greg's furrowed brow stayed on Kevin.

"Dad!"

"Okay." He shook his head, flipping it back to biphasic. "We're only doing this for a few rounds. We're running out of time with the sedation."

Greg shocked the heart.

Compressions.

Nothing.

Shock.

Compressions.

Nothing.

Pig One was dead.

Kevin collapsed back. Blood soaked his shoelaces.

"Kevin." Greg rose, towering over him. "They're going back to the pig farm later with holes in their chests. They aren't going to survive the day anyway."

"We don't know that."

"We're at least being humane and sedating them. This was your idea. What did you think you were signing up for?"

"We're here to find answers. We found its 'soul,' but we just killed it."

Greg stiffened; he leaned forward. "Then let's not make that mistake again. Let's double-check the defibrillators—"

"Maybe it wasn't the shock," Jasper said. "Remember the patient in Atlanta, and Steven in the cadaver lab? When you die the 'soul' leaves. It must work the other way around. If you remove it for too long, it's fatal."

Greg eyed the remaining pigs. He paced, before rotating Pig Two on the tarp, so it was head to toe with Pig Three. "Once it's out of the body there's a window of fifteen seconds. Enough time to swap them."

They gawked.

"Oh damn. Okay," Jasper said.

Greg turned on the second defibrillator. "Kevin, think you can do a thoracotomy faster than my top resident?"

Jasper smirked, eye level with Kevin. "You ready, old man?"

Kevin's adrenaline surged and washed away his trepidation. He knelt back-to-back with Jasper.

"When you're inside I'll fire both defibrillators," Greg said. "The blue lights have to leave the chests at the same time. Rotate to your left to switch to the other pig. I'll let you know when to rotate. Questions?"

They shook their heads.

"Ready? Go."

Scalpels sliced skin. Scissors cut through thick rib meat.

Kevin cranked the rib spreaders, and a throaty squeal escaped his pig's mouth. "No, no, no!" He flinched. "We need more sedation!"

"I'll do it myself. I'm not letting the supplier back in here." Greg took off his gloves, flicked the ketamine syringe to clear the air bubble, and injected Pig Three's rump. After a minute the pig's whimpers went silent. "Keep going. Open the cavity wider, you're almost there."

Kevin, fighting back nausea, leaned into his final turn of the rib spreaders.

"You're both on sustained setting." Greg watched their paddles slide into place. "Ready?!" He deployed the shocks.

"Got it!" Kevin said.

"Me too!" Jasper tried to steady his trembling hands.

The pair of rippling blue energies hovered within feet of each other.

"Okay, rotate!" Greg said.

They turned in synchrony.

"Good ... steadyyy," Greg said.

They found the opposing chest and leaned in.

"Maybe just separate your hands."

The paddles parted; the blue lights erupted in brilliant flashes, then quickly faded.

They stared at each other. Jasper dropped his scalding paddles in a cooking pan. "What—"

"Wait." Greg's eyes darted between the two pigs. They were still breathing, and the hearts were beating. He focused on their legs. "Come on. Come on."

They started moving.

Kevin looked to his father, who was smiling at him. It had been years since he felt it. *Acceptance.*

Then the blood drained from Kevin's face.

His favorite blue eyes were over Greg's shoulder. *Grace.*

Greg followed his gaze. No one moved.

"What?" Grace swallowed. "What's happening here?"

Kevin stood.

She regarded him with horror. "I wanted to hear about your trip, but you avoided me all week, and now ... this." She clutched her stomach.

Kevin's bloody gloves dropped to his feet. He stepped towards her; Greg held out his hand, stopping him.

Grace took a breath. "I shouldn't be here." She hurried inside, in tears.

20. SEQUELA

Kevin sidestepped his father and went after her. "Grace!"

His bloody shoes stopped on the kitchen floor. She saw their trail.

"What the hell is going on? Please say something!" she said.

"I'm so sorry you saw this. I haven't called because ... we ... Baby, we discovered something in Atlanta that could help Alex, but I can't ... We signed non-disclosure agreements."

Grace stepped back, searching the stranger in front of her. She wrapped her jacket tighter. "I'm guessing it has to do with the blue light you just pulled out of that butchered pig?"

His shoulders dropped. "I ..." He tried to think of what to say, of how to start.

"Kevin. Please."

Her fear and distress paralyzed him.

She heard muffled squeals and flinched. "What are you doing?"

He flushed.

"Really? Nothing?"

Remember why you're here. This is for Alex. "I can't."

Grace's eyes fell on the photo from his white coat ceremony; Greg beaming in pride at his son. "I'm out of here."

She quickly turned the corner and went out the front door. Her seatbelt was on by the time Kevin reached the doorway.

She looked back.

This was his moment to chase after her, to explain, to reassure; but he stood still, silent, and watched her pull away.

The street was empty and so was he.

The road went out of focus. He shifted down to his feet, dismayed by their inaction.

Whispers floated to his ears from behind him. He turned and saw Greg and Jasper stop mid-sentence. Greg motioned toward the dining room.

Kevin slowly closed the door. He somehow found them through his haze and sat in the corner.

The phone rang at exactly 3 pm. Steven was ecstatic. They had received full consent from a patient's father for the procedure and he even signed the non-disclosure agreement.

Apparently, anything they could've done to his son "would be an improvement." They shocked him with fifty joules of biphasic energy, the same as Katherine Trudy, and he woke up and told his father he loved him for the first time in ten years.

Kevin could only watch as Greg and Jasper recounted their day, adding to the excitement. It was all distant, inaccessible.

"Our predictions are confirmed," Steven said. "Biphasic energy changes the 'soul' and monophasic allows it to be moved. Working with pigs I guess there's no way to know if monophasic changes it too, but we're pulling this together here."

Kevin tried to process the information, but Grace was seeping into his senses. He heard her whisper; he smelled her hair. He was losing her.

"Steven, can you hold a moment?" Greg hit the mute button. "Kevin, why don't you step out and take some time? A lot's happened today."

I'm out of here, her voice echoed.

She's alone. Suffering. This can't be how it ends.

Kevin pushed himself to his feet. "I have to see her."

Greg splayed his fingers on the table. He gripped it tightly. "What you say to her- Steven?" He confirmed the phone was still on mute. "What you say to her can have huge consequences."

"I don't think she'd say anything."

"Stay here. I need you to focus. We're close to finishing this," Greg said. "Then once we're done and Alex is better, you'll have plenty of time to reconnect with her. She's a great person, but she's not family."

Kevin winced. He slumped against the wall, as something disturbingly powerful coursed through him.

Greg's hands went limp. "I didn't mean—"

Kevin was down the front steps before he could finish. *Get to her. Now.*

He flew out of Long Grove at lightspeed. Call. No answer. Call. No Answer. *I have to fix this!* The smoke dissipated and he was in her hallway. It was longer than he remembered.

And he had no idea what he was going to say.

He cautiously approached her door and knocked. It opened. Grace's roommate, Jen.

She blocked the doorway, sizing up her adversary. "She's not here."

"Please. I'm here to make things right."

"And you came empty-handed?"

Kevin nodded. "No stops along the way. Couldn't waste another moment."

Jen's arm slid off the doorframe. She righted herself. "Roof." Her eyes lowered. "Nice shoes."

He bounded up three flights of stairs; his blood-stained sneakers stepped out onto stone tiles. Dormant lights zig zagged overhead. An unlit fireplace was nestled in a wall behind glass, encircled by empty furniture. Behind it all was Grace, sitting on a ledge, backlit by the sinking sun.

He approached; his movements carefully chosen. "Can I sit with you?"

She paused. Nodded.

"I had to be here." He joined her on the ledge and took in her face.

She stayed on him. A tear fell, uninterrupted.

"I can always see your light. Even after ..." Kevin's words crumbled; they left with the wind. He shook his head.

"Can't hide who I am. Not fair to anyone," she said.

The din of the city below filled their space. A minute passed.

Her hands slid down her jeans. "Do you really think we can continue on like this?"

"I want to be with you."

Grace stopped on his hands, white knuckling on the ledge. "Your son needs you, and I can't get in the way of that. I don't want to make things harder than they already are."

"No. You've always been an amazing, positive force."

"That changed this week." She stood, her cheek now dry. "You've kept something from me and it's poisoning us. This is where it's left us."

"Grace, I ..."

"I know you. I *see* you. And I saw you there, covered in pig's blood. You knew what you were doing was wrong." Her face hardened. "Then, you let me go."

I never meant to hurt you, Grace. You're the only one I want to share any of this with.

She was across a widening divide, shrouded in her disappointment and anger. There was only one way to reach her. *Come from love. Trust my truth.*

He told her. Everything.

Atlanta, the other patients, biphasic, monophasic, the soul, everything gushed out. She listened, wide-eyed, as he purged months of suppressed fear and helplessness.

A gentler quiet returned.

Grace closed her eyes. They slowly opened on the dark fireplace. She walked to the wall switch and turned it on, before sitting on a couch to take in the blue flames.

He joined her. "Do you believe me?"

"I do," she whispered. "Thank you for telling me." She leaned over and hugged him. Her hand stopped for a moment on his chest then returned to her side. "Your dad blames himself for what happened to Alex. He's driven by guilt and you're along for the ride now."

"And the further I go, the more it consumes me, but what choice do I have? He's my son."

"This isn't just about your family. It's so much more than that." She returned to the fire. "If all of this is true, you're *changing peoples' souls* without speaking to the patients. They're losing control of their own lives."

"But these patients had already lost control. They were too sick to give consent."

"And that gives you the right to decide who they'll become?"

Behind the swirling air, in the dark recess of the fireplace Kevin saw his younger, idealistic self, learning the tenets of medical ethics in his new white coat. Are you proud of me now?

"You're right," he whispered.

"This isn't a test. It's not about being 'right' anymore. It's about your actions. They have consequences." Grace's lip trembled. Something was breaking inside her. "I understand completely, but I can't go down this path with you."

His heart plummeted.

"I'm so sorry," she cried.

"But we can make changes, we can figure out a way to consent the patients like you said. Once we fix Alex this will all be over."

"Kevin, this is sacred. This box should've never been opened, but it is now."

"Please don't do this. We can make this work. I love you."

"And I love you too, but sometimes that's not enough." She smiled with a confidence that obliterated him. "I'll never say anything. I promise."

Kevin was scorched earth. A forgotten desert town. The kind that families drive through on a road trip and wonder what happened there.

"I think it's time you go."

His shattered face pleaded, searching for any hint of a way back in, but there was nothing. Gone.

Kevin felt his body somehow leave the roof and make it downstairs to his car. He collapsed in the driver's seat and shut the door.

The nightmare was real. He was radioactive. "FUCKKKK!!!" He smashed the armrest and ripped it from its hinge.

A couple on the sidewalk peeked inside. They quickly left.

His phone rang. Dad. He rejected the call.

It rang again.

Kevin matched his breathing to it. He answered.

"Please talk to me. Are you okay?" Greg asked.

"Not okay," Kevin snipped.

"Where are you? What do you need?"

"It's over, Dad."

Kevin heard him exhale. It wasn't shared misery, it wasn't helplessness, it was relief.

"I'm really sorry," Greg said. "What happened?"

His eyes narrowed. *Shut this down. No more questions.* "I broke up with her," he lied.

"All of this is so complicated. I hate that this had to happen." He paused and Kevin prayed he wouldn't say another word. "Did you tell her anything?"

"No."

Test Subject 2
Interaction 8
Ford Hospital
051300SMAY19

Informed Consent for Pneuma Transplant

<u>Today we will be assessing whether you:</u>
[X] Understand the transplant process including the procedural details, risks, benefits, and alternatives
[] Express a choice on whether to proceed consistent with your preferences and values
[X] Appreciate the consequences of participating or refusing
[] Show appropriate reasoning when comparing these consequences

[X]: Denotes the objective has been completed
[]: Denotes the objective is still pending

This interaction is being video recorded.

———

I open the door and smell Mom's perfume again.
"I'm not your fucking puppet. Cut it out or I walk."
"I know this must be difficult. Please." He nods at my chair from across the table.
The door closes behind me. I don't move.

"You understand this procedure, but we're not convinced that you think you have a problem let alone one that needs fixing."

"I'm here, aren't I?"

"You're here because you're miserable and since your memory's intact, you know you were happy at one point with your family. But beyond that, I'm not sure, are you?"

I ... can't focus. The perfume's overpowering. "Did you hear me? Stop."

I feel her in the room now, with Dad. Their heads are down.

"None of this is your fault, but now you have three personality traits: defiance, complete self-absorption, and lack of insight, that block your processing. They're your 'locked doors.'" He stands to meet me. "We broke through them during the last session. You felt it."

Another wave hits. *I gaze at my parents longingly.* I'm lightheaded. I lower myself into the chair.

He probes. "Can you tell me your diagnosis?"

"Antisocial personality disorder."

"In your own words."

"I use people, I hurt them, and I don't give a shit."

Mom looks at me.

"Do you believe that's a problem?"

She moves closer. She's yelling. That bitch. Wait, she's begging me.

"Do you believe that's a problem?" he repeats.

She looks tortured. Lost. What have I done to you? I'm sorry. I'm so sorry. "Yes." I curl forward. "I can't keep hurting them."

"Who?"

"My family."

He lets out a slow breath, glancing back at the mirror with a smile. "Do you think this procedure could benefit you?"

"Fuck if I know. But it could, I guess."

"This is my last question. If you answer it, then the consent process is complete. If this procedure works, why will you be better than you are now?"

I close my eyes. "I won't be alone."

21. LAKEFILL

The blurry fireball dove and crashed into Kevin's shin. "Fuck, James!" He dropped to a knee, squeezing his throbbing flesh. "How about a heads up?!"

James walked over and picked up the baseball. "You could never catch my curve."

Kevin grimaced and sat. *Let's add an injury to the shit cocktail. Fan-fucking-tastic.*

James dropped his glove next to Kevin and stared past him down the man-made peninsula. Scattered bundled college kids, mostly high, were engrossed in the white-capped lake. "How was Operation: Pigs in a Blanket? Did it help what's-his-name?"

Kevin paused, finding his cover story. "Jasper? Sadly, someone had already tried that thoracotomy approach in some obscure article we missed. It was still helpful, though. Thanks, again, for the pigs."

"You can thank my Navy mentor. The SEAL teams still use pigs for their medical resuscitations." James joined him on the grass. He gripped the ball tightly, digging his thumbnail into the raised seam. "I know you've had a tough time recently, but I have a 'good news, bad news' kind of thing. I wanted to tell you in person."

Kevin slumped. "Let's get the bad news over with."

"Judy had a heart attack."

"Oh, shit. Is she okay?!"

"It happened a few days ago. She's in heart failure."

He saw Judy's face behind the bar. She'd survived so much hardship, yet she was full of compassion and always focused on whoever she was with. Always giving.

"Where is she now?" Kevin asked.

"Saint Monica."

She's at Grace's hospital. Kevin felt ice in his spine. He lay on it, breaking into a cold sweat.

"Are you okay, Sticks? Sorry man, I didn't know how to bring it up."

I can't lose Judy too. Tingling gloves encased Kevin's hands. "I ... just need a moment." He fought against his constricting chest. *Make it stop.*

James watched him writhe. He reached into his pocket, flipped open his lighter, and held it above Kevin who groaned upon seeing the flame. *That's not helping!* It transported him to Grace's rooftop where he relived their final moment together by the fireplace.

"I've had these too. You're okay." James directed Kevin back to the glow. "Stay right here. Find your breath."

Kevin squinted, willing himself to focus on the flickering light. *Stay on it ... Steady ... Burn it all ... Then begin again.*

Just like Grace did. She moved on.

And I have to do the same. I have to let her go now.

He took a deep drag of cool air ... Then again ... And felt his senses settle. Calming, warm sunlight reached his skin through the tree branches.

"Judy's giving you *The Nightcap*, isn't she?"

James flipped the lighter shut. He nodded.

Kevin braced himself on his elbows. "Wow. Sorry it happened this way."

"It obviously hasn't sunk in yet." James ripped up a handful of grass. "When did these panic attacks start?"

"After Grace left."

The blades fell between his fingers.

"Do you still get them?" Kevin asked.

"No."

"How'd you get over them?"

James tapped his lighter. "Meditation, and I left home."

The final stragglers mounted their scooters and rolled away. They were alone. The air vibrated.

"I thought I knew Grace pretty well, then she told me she left you for someone else. That girl would've done *anything* for you." James faced him. "Even lie for you."

Kevin's pupils dilated. *Interrogation. James's specialty.*

James sized up Kevin's injured leg through the eyes of a hunter. "What happens between you two isn't my business, but she's one of my closest friends and she's not talking to me anymore. Did you do something?"

Kevin shielded his leg underneath him. His guilt loosened the reins on his tongue. "Are you asking if I cheated on her? No."

James swelled. "We talked about keeping things from each other. Now's the time."

"I ... I was shocked too. She must have met this new guy at her hospital. She—"

"I stopped by to see Greg a few days ago. He said you broke up with her. Try again."

Kevin scrambled in his corner. "She broke up with me and I was embarrassed. I told Dad I ended it, so he would stop asking questions."

"Why did she end it? And you can drop the 'other guy' crap. She wouldn't do something like that."

Kevin's gears grounded to a halt. His teeth fused together.

"And you're lying to Greg now? What's going on with you?"

He looked at James. *I just told Grace everything and look where it got me. Maybe someday I can explain.*

James leaned in, stunned by his silence. "Really?"

Kevin faced forward, fighting against his inner torment, but his mind was made up. *I can't tell you. I'm sorry.*

James slowly unclenched his fists. He followed Kevin's gaze to the horizon where the lake blended with the sky. *Their own private ocean.*

"I don't know about you, but I think about the championship a lot ... and how beaten down you were heading into it," James said. "Your mom was spiraling with her drinking, and it was so fucked up between you and Greg. You were a mess. Then the big game finally came, tied in the last inning. It was my moment. He threw a pitch I should've hit into the next county, but the bat stayed on my shoulder. Struck out. It killed me."

He rolled the baseball to Kevin. "But then you came to the plate, and you knocked it out of the park. You did it.

You were the hero when all the cards were against you. You were my hero."

James got up and left his glove on the ground. He started down the walkway. "Give my glove to Alex. You can find your way home, right?"

22. ROLL CALL

Side ... To side ... To side ... To side.

Kevin watched Alex inch a chocolate easter egg across the tray table. Side ... To side ... To side ...

"Mom should leave."

"She'll never do that," Kevin said.

"Staying is going to kill her."

"It might Alex. How'd that make you feel?"

Alex paused, registering his father's irritation. "I think I'd be sad, then I wouldn't feel much. The feelings don't last long."

Kevin channeled his remaining shred of strength. *Reach him. We're running out of time. They'll be back soon.*

He held Alex's limp hand next to his diaper. "There's something important we need to talk about."

"Not the feeding tube. All everyone does is argue about it. Useless," Alex said.

"There's another way we can help you. Alex, you're not crazy. You know that, right?"

His son stared blankly at him.

"Remember how much you loved music? You had calluses on your fingers from playing guitar for hours."

He nodded.

"You were enthusiastic, creative. Remember when you first woke up in the hospital you told me you felt something was wrong? You told me, 'There's nothing here.'"

Alex drifted out the window. "Yes."

Kevin swallowed. His son's monochromatic world seemed to veil the final golden hues of the day. He leaned towards Alex. "Your personality was changed when you were attacked. That's why you can't feel emotions and why you don't care."

He looked at his father. "I don't understand."

"We discovered personality is located in there." Kevin pointed to the scar on his emaciated chest. "When they saved you, they accidentally changed you."

Alex pulled his hand away. "Who did this?"

Kevin froze. "I …" He heard footsteps in the hall. The door opened, but he couldn't turn away from Alex's face.

Susan appeared in the room, glaring at Kevin as she joined Alex on the bed. Greg followed with Steven and Aaron, who sat near Alex's feet.

"Hi Alex." Aaron smiled warmly. "We're friends of your dad and grandpa. We came all the way from Atlanta to meet you."

"Hi," Alex said, but he appeared to be focused on his mother's smeared eyeliner. He closed his eyes and breathed deeply.

Kevin reached for his hand again and held on tight. "I spoke with Alex about his personality, about what happened to him."

Everyone was still.

"What did you say?" Greg asked.

"I know I'd love to hear it." Susan's danger vein was growing. "I'm so glad you're sharing all this valuable information now. I just learned so much from Greg." Her voice was acidic.

Kevin lowered his eyes. "You have every right to be angry."

Her fingers were covered in Band-Aids. Dried blood.

"I thought it was time to tell—"

"Grandpa, did you do this to me?" Alex fixed on Greg.

Greg spun round to see Kevin, mouth open.

Kevin's hands came up. "I didn't—"

"No, honey." Susan rubbed her son's hair, her cold face now turned towards Greg. "It was an accident. They don't know who did it."

Greg leaned forward, hands on his knees, head down.

She continued, "But they know how to fix you with a surgery, how to make you better."

She addressed Aaron, softening, "How many people were changed like him?"

"We've had three great outcomes, as recently as last week," Steven replied.

His confidence was palpable, fresh off the third success story using fifty joules.

Kevin's mind quickly became clinical. *Three patients. That's not sufficient evidence to tear open my son's chest again.* No sooner did his fearful thoughts escalate than he became mindful of his son's hand cradled in his. And he could only feel skin and bones. *There's nothing left of him, inside or out.*

Kevin shook his head. "My family deserves to know about the other patients."

Steven adjusted his glasses. "There were three more. One woman awoke with a similar personality to Alex, but she left the hospital with her family, and we can't find her. One didn't survive the trauma. The last was a child." Steven glanced at Greg. "He became disturbed and died in the hospital."

"Oh, God." Susan moved back, picking at the bandages on her ravaged fingers.

"It was early in the process, the first and only time they used that energy setting," Greg said. "There hasn't been an outcome like that since."

"Right. All the patients that received fifty joules became very pleasant. That's what we would use on Alex," Steven said.

Susan searched her son's face. "Will he be the same as before? Will he be Alex again?"

"He wouldn't have certain undesirable traits anymore," Steven said.

"The severe, pathologic apathy that's keeping him here," Aaron added.

Greg stood and walked over to her. "Susan, anything would be an improvement," he whispered.

She gently rubbed Alex's arm. "Have you been listening?"

"What do you think about all this?" Kevin asked.

"Too many people. Too much talking. I don't care." Alex pulled the blanket up to his chin.

"They're talking about a surgery," Kevin said. "Once you're unconscious, they would go inside your chest and change your personality, which may help you feel better and more like yourself. Would you like to leave this room? This may be a way to go home."

"I'm fine here."

Kevin pressed on, "You're an adult now and if you can show us that you understand, then you get to make your own decision about this. Remember what we just talked about? We can help you return to how you were before. Would you like that? You'll be able to take care of yourself."

Alex gazed at his mother. His lips opened, then closed.

A tear fell down Susan's cheek. "Do it," she said to Steven.

"I just want to make sure ..." Kevin stammered. "If you could give me more time with him I could—"

Greg held up his hand. He addressed Susan. "I think that's the right call."

"You wish to proceed?" Steven asked.

Susan nodded.

"Great," Steven said. "I'll go grab the paperwork." He left.

Kevin stood. *Alex, please. Show me you know what's going on.* "Dad, Alex is right here. Give him time to grasp this!"

Greg ignored him, taking Susan aside. "He's a great surgeon. He would go right through Alex's old scar. It would take less than thirty—"

"Dad!"

Greg stopped. He advanced towards Kevin, his words a blend of whisper and snarl. "This is happening. No more delays. No more wasting time."

Kevin leaned around him, imploring Susan. "Alex doesn't understand. There's risk and—"

"Kevin, please," she said. "Look at what he's become."

"Enough," Greg said.

Kevin returned to full height. "He deserves better." He stayed, looking into Greg's hardened eyes.

"Enough," Greg repeated.

Kevin left the room, only to find his feet slow in the rubble of his righteous intentions.

Steven came around the corner and quickly ended his phone call. "Updated Clarissa. Step out to get some air?"

"Something like that."

"Coming back inside?"

"Not yet."

Steven approached Alex's room and stopped. "You think I don't listen to your input, but I do. I agree with gaining consent from the patients," he said quietly.

"Then why didn't you do it? You just bypassed Alex in there."

"It's complicated now."

"Complicated? This is my son and we're rushing through this. This should be his call, at least give him a chance!"

Steven glanced inside before beckoning Kevin away from the doorway.

"There's a growing sentiment in the group to jump at this opportunity while the window's open."

"With you at the helm."

"Kevin, we waited *five years*. Do you really think I'm at the helm?"

Kevin went quiet. He reached for the handrail and leaned against the wall. "Of course, it's him. Always is."

There was a slow crescendo of rhythmic squeaking. An orderly appeared pushing a patient in a wheelchair past them. Her eyes were on the ceiling, mouth open, drooling.

"What if Alex ends up like that?" Kevin asked.

"He's not far from that now. Desperate times."

"Fuck, what if he dies?"

"He won't. I have the best survival outcomes in the state."

Kevin studied him; for the first time, his confidence was welcome.

Steven straightened, challenging Kevin to do the same. "Come back inside with me."

Kevin followed him into the room.

Steven handed Susan the surgical consent forms. They waited for her to finish signing.

"Where's the facility director?" Aaron asked.

"When you enter the lobby it's the last door on your left, Dr. Abrahams," she said.

Aaron tucked the forms in his pocket and addressed Susan, "You're his designated surrogate, so please come with me and follow my lead. Kevin, would you like to join?"

"Yes, of course."

"Good. Remember, after this is over, Alex won't need a surrogate anymore. Ready to get him out of here?" Aaron smiled at her.

She exhaled. "Yes."

He paused on her face.

"Yes," she repeated firmly.

He handed her a pair of gloves.

"What're these ..." Susan paused, embarrassed by her dirty bandages. She acquiesced, sliding them on with a flinch.

"Give us twenty minutes," Aaron said.

They returned in ten.

"Alex is no longer subject to involuntary admission. Here's the discharge notice. He can leave now," Aaron said to Greg and Steven.

Susan walked over to the bed, exhausted. "I can't believe you're a doctor and a lawyer."

"Long nights at the library," Aaron said.

She smiled faintly.

"That's it for us," Steven said. "We'll meet you at Valley Green. We have to finalize everything for Alex's surgery."

He departed with Aaron.

After a long silence, Susan moved closer to Kevin. "You promised me you'd fix this, remember?"

He nodded slowly and put his arm around her shoulders. They gazed at their boy together.

Greg watched them from the bench. He stood and made his way out, stopping to place three plane tickets on the table. "This happens tomorrow."

Test Subject 1
Interaction 7
Ford Hospital
060900SMAY19

Informed Consent for Pneuma Transplant

Today we will be assessing whether you:
[X] Understand the transplant process including the procedural details, risks, benefits, and alternatives
[X] Express a choice on whether to proceed consistent with your preferences and values
[X] Appreciate the consequences of participating or refusing
[X] Show appropriate reasoning when comparing these consequences

[X]: Denotes the objective has been completed
[]: Denotes the objective is still pending

This interaction is being video recorded.

———

Travis stands to leave, but I'm not ready for him to go.
"Please stay a moment. This is likely the last time I'll see you."
He slowly lowers his bag and sits, avoiding eye contact. "Sorry Ms. Trudy. I've never been good with goodbyes."

"I've been such a chatterbox these last few days. Tell me about yourself. Is there a woman in your life?"

He blushes. "No ma'am. Just focused on my career right now."

"You're doing a great job."

"Thank you."

"Have you always wanted to be a healer?"

His brown eyes darken. "No, I came to it after college. My closest friend was shot in the chest at our graduation party, and I couldn't do anything to help him. It changed my path."

My scar burns with sympathy. "Did he survive?" I whisper.

He shakes his head.

"Oh, Travis." I sigh, struggling to find a place to settle. "In an instant everything changed for you. So much pain, but you found a beautiful career as a result."

His eyes finally reach mine.

"I went through something similar. The gunshot that took me down also started me on this whole trajectory, and I changed too, completely. You could say I was reborn. Now, I'm so grateful I get to cherish moments like this."

He smiles.

There you are. "I admire you, Travis. You have a big heart." My chest tightens. I cough.

He darts to his bag and grabs the nebulizer.

I wave him off. "Told you I was talking too much. I'll be okay."

We both wait for the wheezes to subside. "Have you always lived here in Chicago?"

"My whole life," he says.

"I love this city. I was born here. I was crushed when my father moved us to Atlanta, and we never came back. I think he was trying to escape his past."

Travis falls silent. He touches the metal cross around his neck. "The sins of the fathers." A series of blinks bring him back into the room.

What a sensitive young man with this vulnerable side. I can trust him.

I reach into my purse. "I want you to have this, to say thank you. I'm so grateful for the care you've given me."

He glows with appreciation. "So thoughtful of you, but I don't think-"

"You can and you will. It'll be our little secret." I smile.

He regards the envelope carefully, "Thank you," and slides it onto his clipboard.

"Travis, can I ask a favor of you?"

"Yes."

"I have another envelope. Can you please give it to the other participant after the procedure?"

He pushes the air as if I'd just tried to kiss him. "I've been given strict instructions that you're not allowed to interact with him."

"My dear, this is for *after* the procedure. It won't change a thing."

"Why me? Why not give it to the supervisors?"

"Because I'm quite fond of you and I know you won't read it." I lean on my elbow. "Please, Travis. The last wish of a dying woman."

He can't hold my gaze. His head drops and he extends his hand.

"Thank you." I give it to him.

He nods and leaves for the door. "I'm going to miss you."

"I wish you a wonderful life. You have so much to be grateful for."

Mr. Montoya passes him in the doorway and enters to find my last envelope waiting for him.

"Oh! I found the perfect window down the hall. It overlooks the skyline. Absolutely breathtaking," I say.

"There's an even better view upstairs before you enter the operating room."

"Good, I want that to be the last thing I see."

I breathe in. No wheeze. No cough. *I'm ready.*

23. PASSAGE

Kevin saw blurry light in the corner of his eye. He lifted his cheek off the ... asphalt? What the fuck?

His body was freezing; his head was warm ... and wet. Then the pain hit hard. He grabbed his throbbing skull only to quickly pull his hand away. It was bloody.

He swayed onto his feet and peered down the empty alleyway. The world tilted; he grabbed a chain-link fence, stumbling towards the light. It was an open door.

He got as far as a neighboring wall and vomited. A lot. His feeble attempt to wipe his mouth sent him reeling inside. He collapsed to the floor, coughing, as dust whipped up into his face.

"No, no. Get out!" a woman shouted above him. "Charlie! Someone came through the back." She dropped closer. "What ... Are you okay?"

He was rolled onto his side.

"It's a kid. Get a fresh rag. Is anyone out there?!"

Footsteps around him.

"I don't see anyone."

His double vision became singular. A frightened face under thick black bangs was looking at him.

"What's your name?" she asked.

"Kevin."

She pulled him upright. "What happened?"

He sat cross-legged. They were in a storage closet. Old shelves. Old table. Everything dusty.

"I came here to get away from ... To just get away and ... I was walking down the street and these guys grabbed me and took me into the alley. It happened so fast."

Wait ... He reached into his jacket. His wallet was gone.

"I'm so sorry. Is there anyone we can call? Your parents?"

Kevin shook his head; the ache intensified. "My mom's dying. I couldn't be in the hospital anymore."

Her wide eyes were awash with concern as she was handed a towel. "I'm guessing you don't want to go to the hospital now."

He started to shake his head again and stopped himself. "Can I stay here?"

"Are you twenty-one?"

"At midnight."

A small smile flashed across her face. She looked back at the man and held up two fingers. He returned a moment later with two whiskeys then departed, closing the curtain.

She lowered herself to the ground and sat with him. "I'm Judy. Welcome to my bar."

Kevin's eyes opened and a tear crept out. A requiem. *You saved me and now I can't save you.*

Judy was on the hospital bed next to him. Her breathing was shallow and rapid, her face swollen around her nasal cannula. She awoke and saw Kevin. That same small smile returned. "You came."

He nodded and slid his chair closer. There was a rosary in her lap.

"How's your boy?" she asked weakly. "Better than me I hope."

Kevin took a deep breath. "We're taking him to Atlanta to see specialists tonight. They may be able to help."

"Good news. I'll send prayers."

"Thank you."

"It's hard enough being a father, but you have the burden of being his doctor too. Who's taking care of you?"

He found her kind eyes. "I don't know."

"You have to put your oxygen mask on first before helping others do the same, doc. Alex has a team now. Please get one too. They miss you."

Kevin looked away. He drifted to the back room with James, hearing Grace's name for the first time.

"James is sad. Some of that's for me, but losing you has been hard on him. He doesn't have much, Kevin, and although inside he has everything that matters, he needs you. And you need him." Judy paused to catch her breath. She grabbed her rosary and held it firmly. "Your girlfriend came by too."

Grace was here. He searched for traces of her, but there was nothing.

"We broke up, Judy."

"I know. It's a shame. That woman is very much in love with you." She took a deep drag from her nasal cannula. "But only you know what's right for you. Your inner voice has to lead."

Kevin nodded at her rosary. "Is that the voice you listen to?"

"Is there a difference?" She reached for him. "Some things will always be there for you no matter how hard you push them away."

Kevin took her hand in his and kissed it. "You are so loved. Rest well. I'll come back and see you after Atlanta."

She squeezed his hand. "Don't tell James, but I always liked your hair the most."

Kevin left her room, and hours later, he left Chicago. When he turned on his phone in Atlanta, a voicemail was waiting for him: a sad physician with a nondescript message asking him to return the call.

Judy had left as well.

Thank you for your light. Thank you for always leaving the door open for me.

Kevin's moment of silence lasted until they arrived at Valley Green.

They stepped out under the night sky and slowly plodded toward the entrance. Jasper ran ahead to grab a wheelchair while Greg trailed behind them in case Alex collapsed backwards. Supported between his parents, Alex was swimming in his old clothes. A journey within a journey, they made it through security.

Then things moved quickly. They gathered in the conference room at 11 p.m. to cover logistics. Aaron would get a baseline assessment of Alex in pre-op; Steven would perform the surgery; Clarissa would provide anesthesia.

No techs, one trusted nurse in the recovery room. They were the only surgery scheduled.

Before long, Alex's faux operation popped on the board, "internal fixation of rib fractures," and everyone took their places. He was wheeled away to OR 1, and, at midnight, Steven's blade entered his skin.

Steven's heart raced as he descended through scar tissue. *The first repeat 'soul' surgery. Incredible.*

His excitement wasn't shared. Clarissa kept her focus on the cardiac monitor.

"How are we doing?" Steven reached for the scissors.

"Good."

"And you?"

She rotated to him. "Also, good."

"Ready to make history again?"

Clarissa nodded.

Steven was acutely aware of the distance between them in the empty room. *You've been on edge ever since your faith was challenged. I'll save this chat for another day. Back to business.*

He secured the rib spreaders in place and cranked the callused ribs open.

Alex's arms tensed up.

"He's moving," Steven said.

Clarissa smothered his pain with boluses of fentanyl and propofol while Steven took the opportunity to double check the biphasic defibrillator. Within a minute blue light illuminated inside Alex's chest.

Fifty joules. Excited to finally meet you, Alex.

He was taken to the recovery room not long after, where his parents and grandfather received him.

"It went well. No surprises." Steven lowered his mask with a smile. "We'll be down the hall in the conference room. Aaron will come later for the post-op evaluation."

"Thank you," they collectively breathed, exchanging hopeful glances.

Then they waited.

———

Muffled sounds reached Alex.

He searched the dark depths around him. *I know this place.*

A light overhead rippled in his periphery; he was gliding up towards it. He surfaced under the moon and a starless night sky.

At first, he heard it. Then he felt it.

He turned to see the ocean was on fire.

24. WORKING TITLE

"Hi Dad."

Kevin looked up. Alex's droopy eyelids were open halfway. *He's smiling.*

Kevin went to him and gently touched his arm. "Hi."

Susan joined them, wiping a tear off her joyful face. "How are you feeling?"

"High," Alex said.

"I bet. We're so glad you're okay. We were told the procedure went well."

"Good." Alex cautiously took a deep breath and moved his left arm. Satisfied his pain was bearable, he pressed a button, raising the head of his bed. Greg came into view. "Grandpa."

"Hi Alex." Greg struggled to contain his emotion.

Kevin closed his eyes, allowing comfort to flow through him. *Alex, you're here. I can feel you again.*

"And who are you?" Alex's cadence slowed.

Kevin opened his eyes to see a nurse approach.

"I'm Christina." She tucked a strand of wavy blonde hair back under her headband and checked Alex's IV fluids.

"You're a pretty one." Alex's eyes dropped lower.

She shifted uncomfortably and shot the Bishops a probing glance.

"Make sure you keep the meds coming," Alex said.

"Will do. Would you like another blanket?"

"No. Leave now."

Christina took a moment to summon her professionalism. "You got it," she said through tight lips and returned to her computer.

Susan's arms folded. "Honey, don't you think you're being harsh? She's here to help."

Alex stared at his mother's reddening face.

Flustered, she found her seat.

Kevin sat between Susan and Greg. His father was rocking back and forth.

Kevin put his arm on Greg's shoulder. "Dad?"

Greg shook away the haze. His misty eyes found Kevin. "It's over. He's finally okay."

Kevin squeezed him.

"I've sat on this for too long and I can't anymore. I need to tell him."

Kevin squeezed harder, trying to get his attention. *Now's not the time.*

Greg missed the cue. "Alex, I'm so sorry. Your first operation. It was me. I ran your resuscitation."

Alex stiffened.

"Your heart stopped and when I went to shock it, I slipped, and shocked an area next to your heart. You've been different ever since."

"What do you mean 'an area next to my heart?'" He turned to Kevin. "Is this the personality thing you were talking about?"

"It was your soul," Greg said.

Alex's face warped. He leaned forward with a wince, examining them. "Wait, you're being serious? My soul?"

They didn't move.

He inhaled, eyes wide on Greg. "My soul??"

Greg's head fell. "I changed it."

"Grandpa was trying to save your life," Kevin said.

"But who was I? *What* was I? I sat in that psych ward for months, not giving a shit about anything and you kept this from me?!"

"We didn't think you could process it," Greg croaked, "and I didn't want to hurt you more than I already had."

Kevin slid to the edge of his seat. "I tried—"

"*Fuck*!" Alex erupted.

Kevin watched his son's emotions surge out of hibernation. A maelstrom of energy swept through him, as he grunted and pushed himself further upright, snapping to Susan. "And you lied to me. You said they didn't know who did it."

Susan covered her face in confusion and shame.

"It was me," Greg repeated. "I've had to live with it every day, but now you're better. You're back."

Kevin went to his son, but Alex kept him at arm's distance. His pulsating hands curled into fists below his seething face.

"Are you back, Alex?" Kevin asked.

He scoured the room, as if searching for something to pummel ... then he saw his reflection.

It took his breath away. His hand glided over his cheekbones.

The fire went out.

Alex turned to his father, who helped lower him back down. "Yeah. I'm back."

Greg clasped his hands. He leaned forward into his thankful palms.

Kevin took in his son's dazed expression, gently moving aside strands of his hair. He unfurled the sheet and tucked him in, and then he felt her. *Grace, you were right. And I have to know.* "I'm sorry, we should have told you sooner. Would you have wanted that?"

Alex stared past him. "I knew something was wrong with me, but I couldn't ... I don't know."

Greg glared at Kevin. "Why are you—"

"You don't get to say anything. You did this," Alex barked at his grandfather.

Greg went pale. "It was an accident."

Kevin held out his hands. "There's no one to blame here, Alex. It truly was an accident, but we could've handled things differently. It's your life. It's your body. You should've had the chance to—"

"Another time," Susan admonished. "He's been through a lot today."

Alex nodded slowly. His eyes closed. "You're all covering for each other," he whispered.

Greg moved closer and reached for the bed. He reluctantly withdrew upon hearing heavy footsteps behind him.

"Is now a good time?" Aaron asked.

Greg slumped and pushed himself upright. "Go for it," he mumbled.

Susan and Kevin joined him, and they headed to the conference room where Steven, Clarissa, and Jasper received them expectantly.

"Is something wrong?" Steven asked.

They took their seats. Kevin leaned forward. "He's definitely changed. He's more expressive, outspoken, but there's an intensity I've never seen before."

Steven's hands came off the armrests. "This sounds like a win to me. I'm sure there's an adjustment period for all this to reset in him."

"But I don't—"

The door slammed open. Aaron entered, snorted, and spat bloody mucus into the nearest trash can. "Can someone take a look at my nose? I think it's broken."

"What the hell happened?" Greg guided him into a chair and assessed the bones of his face. "Seems okay. Is there an otoscope nearby?"

"Not ideal to go searching for one," Steven said. "The less attention we draw to us, the better."

Kevin handed Aaron his pack of travel Kleenex. "Hold pressure for ten minutes. Do you want to go to the ER?"

"No," Aaron said.

Susan slid closer, desperate for an answer.

"Alex said, 'Unless you're here to give me pain meds or food, leave me alone.'" Aaron paused; no doubt irritated at how unprofessional he sounded holding his nose. "I told him I just wanted to talk ... Ask him some questions. Then he told me to come closer and he punched me."

"He hit you?" Susan exclaimed.

Aaron checked the Kleenex. Still bleeding. "How was he with you?"

Kevin flashed to Steven with growing trepidation. "There were parts of him I recognized, but there were parts I didn't. And the Alex we know would never hurt someone like this. Never."

Susan stood, wide-eyed. "What's going on with him? I'm so sorry, Aaron. That's not okay. I ... I want to talk to him." She beckoned Kevin and turned to Greg, but he couldn't take his eyes off the floor.

"I'll take care of Aaron," Jasper said.

After a quick huddle in the hallway, Kevin and Susan reentered the recovery room. The nurse quickly ended her phone call and approached them with alarm. "Can I speak with you?"

Kevin glanced at Alex who was watching him.

"I was gone for literally two minutes," Christina said rapidly, pointing to the bathroom behind her, "and Dr. ..."

"Coates," Kevin said.

"He was bleeding and he said Alex did it. I'm sorry I wasn't here, but I asked him if he wanted security, and he said no." She paused, nervously tugging her badge. "Do you want me to call security?"

"No. We'll take care of it."

"I'm sorry, again. I'll be here. Just signal me if you need anything."

They went to Alex's bedside. Susan leaned over him. "I understand you're in pain, but why did you hit Dr. Coates? Are you okay?"

Kevin watched him slide lower under the sheet. *He's struggling. It's almost as if he's trying to comfort himself. Or wall us away.*

"You need to apologize," Susan continued. "We don't do that in—"

"You didn't even hear my side of what happened. Dominating me like you always do," Alex retaliated.

Her mouth fell open.

"You need to leave."

Kevin interceded, "Alex, your mom doesn't deserve that. We're here because we love you."

He stayed on her. "Leave."

Susan let out a pained breath. She buried her bandaged hands into her pockets, turning to Kevin, head low. "It's okay." She slowly made her way out the door.

Kevin cautiously sat. He looked deeper. "I can see how hard this is for you. It's horrible that you had another surgery. No wonder you're not yourself yet."

Alex took a ragged deep breath and relaxed back on his pillow. They rested in uneasy silence.

"Can Dr. Coates come ..."

Alex flinched upon hearing his name. "I don't want him near me." He slowly lowered the sheet. "Look what he did to me."

His forearm was red.

"What?!" Kevin stood.

"The pain came back, and I couldn't focus on his questions. He must have thought I was ignoring him. He just grabbed my arm and said, 'Stop wasting my time. You're not going to mess this up for us.' He wouldn't let go. I didn't want to hit him, but I didn't have a choice."

Kevin flagged the nurse and quickly went toward her. "When Dr. Coates was here, did you see anything inappropriate?"

She shook her head. "Dr. Coates seemed tired. That's all."

This doesn't make any sense. "I'll be right back, Alex." Kevin strode toward the conference room.

Aaron, bleeding now resolved, froze upon hearing Kevin's accusation.

"I'm sorry, what?" Susan backed away from Aaron.

Aaron held up his bloody hands. "That didn't happen."

"I've known him for years. Zero chance he did this." Steven stood by his colleague. Clarissa nodded in perplexed agreement.

"I saw his arm," Kevin said.

Susan's eyes bored into Aaron. She went to Kevin's side, as Greg and Jasper joined them, dismayed.

Aaron leaned back in his seat. "I would never do something like that." Then recognition seized him. He exhaled through his mouth. "Do you think he could have done it to himself?"

Kevin and Susan recoiled. "Really?"

"I did not do this," he said firmly, "and it would fit certain personality profiles."

No one moved. The space between them filled with misgivings.

"We need his post-op evaluation," Aaron implored.

"Not gonna happen this trip. He's really triggered," Kevin said.

It was a standoff, and Aaron didn't have anything left in the tank for further cross examinations. He stood and gathered his things.

"This is a mistake," Steven said.

"Things need to cool down and we need some clarity on this." Kevin received nods from his rattled family. "We're getting him out of here."

Test Subject 2
Interaction 9
Ford Hospital
061300SMAY19

Canceled. Test subject absent

25. TAKEOFF

Kevin sank into the grey sectional sofa in the lobby of the Atlanta North Hotel, but he was anything but relaxed. Two days of being at Alex's beck and call had left him frazzled. *I will never take another nurse for granted as long as I live.*

The thought triggered a pang of sorrow. He missed his favorite nurse. Kevin searched through the social media on his phone, but he couldn't find Grace.

Jasper sat next to him and took a swig of Mountain Dew. He saw Kevin's baffled face.

"I thought this was a judge-free zone." Jasper chuckled.

"You like that stuff?"

He shrugged, nodded.

"Well, except for your choice of beverage, I'm continuously impressed by you. You've been with us every step of this journey and we're grateful for your help." Kevin held out his hand. "Thank you. Truly."

Jasper shook his hand and smiled. "I really hope everything works out."

A shadow of concern passed between them.

Kevin changed the subject, "I know you're thinking academics, but I really like my new hospital, Chicago Legacy. I would be happy to get you an interview there. Would be my pleasure to work alongside you."

Jasper leaned back in disbelief. "Wow. That means a lot. Thank you."

"Course."

"I may take you up on that." He offered Kevin a sip of the drink.

"Fuck it." Kevin grabbed the can.

Across the lobby, Alex was in the gift shop with Susan and Greg. They were on opposite sides of a rack, stuck on their respective decisions.

Susan peeked through a gap. "Anything good?" she asked Alex.

"Can't decide." He shifted away from the magazines. "I feel off."

"Want more pain medicine? You're due soon." She came around the rack with Greg.

Alex shook his head in irritation. "Why would you buy a different perfume?" he demanded.

She rolled a small bottle in her hand. "Thought I'd try something new. Lots of change recently. Why not me?"

"Don't be ridiculous." Alex snatched the bottle and put it back on the shelf.

Susan glanced at Greg. "Guess I'll stick to the old stuff then," she said with a strained smile.

Greg nodded at her supportively. *It'll take time, but we'll reach him.* He turned to the rack. "Alex, look who it is." He grabbed a *Sports Illustrated*. Michael Phelps was on the cover. "How about I get this for you? Something for the plane ride?"

Alex ignored him. He peered around the rack at the clerk and dragged his rolling suitcase, leaving the shop.

"I'll be with Dad."

———

Kevin saw him approach. He eased him down next to him, patting his son's knee. "Ready to go home?"

Alex nodded.

"If you need a break from Grandpa's, you're welcome to stay with me. I'd love more time with you."

"Yeah, maybe, but I should get back to LA soon."

Kevin swallowed. "I'm sure you miss your friends. We'll find time."

Alex wrestled off his jacket, moving away from him. He couldn't seem to meet Kevin's eyes.

"Can I see how it's healing?" Kevin asked.

Alex reluctantly extended his arm. The redness was gone, just a few small bruises.

"Looks good." Kevin settled back and stopped. *Small bruises.* He flashed back to Aaron's hands in the cafeteria: they were massive, just like the rest of him.

Sound left the room. His heart started pounding. He slowly studied his son. *Did you do this?*

Alex tucked his arm away. "What's up? You okay?"

"Yeah, yeah, I'm good."

Alex paused, looking at Kevin's face for a moment. He stood. "I need the bathroom." He walked past his mother, who was returning from the checkout counter.

"Honey, don't take too long, we've—"

Alex waved her off.

Susan watched him disappear around the corner, lowering herself onto the couch. "He's so agitated." She handed Alex's boarding pass to Kevin. "Can you throw this in his bag? I'm worried he'll forget it."

Kevin nodded, filled with unease. He unzipped the side pocket of Alex's suitcase. *This is all wrong. Why did we leave the hospital? Maybe if ...*

There were two wallets inside the pocket.

He pulled them out and opened them. Neither were his son's.

"Kevin, what's ...?" Susan's voice failed her.

What's happening? Kevin looked up to see Alex turn the corner. He quickly put the wallets back, but it was too late.

"Dad!!"

Kevin and Susan stood up.

Alex went at Kevin, stopping within inches of his face. "You went through my stuff?!"

"Why do you have other people's wallets in your bag?"

Alex shifted uneasily between his parents. "Back off." He grabbed the handle and moved his suitcase behind him. He saw Jasper stand up behind his father. "And you can get the fuck out of here, this doesn't concern you."

Susan found her voice at last. "Alex!"

Jasper held up his hands. He glanced at Kevin furtively, before moving towards Greg who was frozen at the entrance of the gift shop.

"How could you do this?" Susan's voice cracked.

Alex confronted her. "Those fuckers at UCLA think they can hold me back a year. Watch my friends pass me by. Hell no. I'm out. And since I'll need a job, why not get a jump-start?"

"Stealing?!" Susan exclaimed.

"It's income. And c'mon, they were rich businessmen, they can afford to be taken down a notch."

Kevin stood fast. "Are you really gloating over the crime you just committed?" He held out his hand. "Give them to me. And while you're at it, you can tell me what really happened to your arm."

There was a flicker of fear in Alex's eyes. He broke eye contact. "Get away from me," he said through clenched teeth and took a step back.

Kevin leaned forward; hand still extended. "I'm not going to say it again."

Alex's eyes widened. Two police officers were walking towards him. "Alex Bishop, you're under arrest for theft."

He looked around the room, searching for his accuser. He paused on Jasper and Greg. *You.*

Alex tried to run, but Susan grabbed his arm. "No!"

"Let go!" His fist crashed into her jaw.

Susan's body went limp, and she collapsed to the floor. Her head struck marble.

Alex and Kevin looked down, horrified, as a black wave engulfed them all.

Officers shouting. Flailing limbs.

Greg could hardly take it in. He was reliving the nightmare back outside the trauma bay in the parking lot. The bodies were descending on Alex again, but this time it wasn't to save him. It was to protect everyone else.

What have you become?

The gift shop clerk stood quietly next to Greg, hands folded. "He stole from my customers yesterday. It was on camera."

Greg sighed and closed his eyes.

"Grandpa!" Alex's voice cut through the chaos, as he emerged, purple, grimacing in handcuffs. "They're hurting me," he wailed.

"Alex!" Greg snaked through amateur paparazzi. "Please stop, he just had surgery!"

"Help me!"

Out of reach, Greg made it to the front door to intercept them. "It's going to be okay!"

As Alex was led away, he looked back, his face twisted and swollen. But it was the rage and betrayal that made his grandson truly unrecognizable.

"It's going to be okay," Greg said.

He watched Alex slump in submission against the police officers and disappear with them into the street.

A hush fell over the lobby, then moaning came from the floor. Susan was curled in Kevin's arms.

"Where is he? Where's my boy?" she sputtered, clutching him. "What do ... we do now? What do we do?"

26. Bishop Takes Night

"Your son's in pain and saying he can't breathe. There's blood on his shirt. We're redirecting him to Valley Green Hospital."

Kevin felt numb. He couldn't help but fear the worst. He ended the call with the officer and quickly alerted the last departing paramedic who was loading Susan into the ambulance in front of the hotel.

"Please take her to Valley Green. Her son's about to be a patient there."

The paramedic secured her in place. "Didn't he just hit her? You sure that's a good idea?"

"Please," Susan implored.

He sighed and wiped the sweat off his forehead with his sleeve. He adjusted the collar under her swollen jaw. "As long as you fight to stay awake, I'll get you there. Deal?"

She focused on the swirling metal ceiling above her. "Deal."

As the paramedic closed the double doors, Kevin called to her, "We'll be right behind you. Hang in there."

Kevin watched the ambulance fire up its lights and sirens and part the afternoon traffic. He flagged a cab and turned to Greg and Jasper who were nearby on a bus stop bench.

"Those bastards manhandled Alex. If they ..." Greg could only muster a guttural groan.

Jasper guided Greg to his feet and led him aside, patting his back. He called out to Kevin, "Go. We'll catch up."

Kevin arrived at the hospital minutes later. He bypassed the guards and volunteers, avoiding their confused recognition, and made his way to the emergency department.

He found his son on a gurney handcuffed to the side rail. He was drowsy, *likely from the morphine.* Steven was on a stool, evaluating him. "Hi." He acknowledged Kevin without taking his eyes off the surgical site, blood seeping from the wound.

"Thanks for seeing him so quickly," Kevin said.

"Of course. I'm on call anyway." Steven plucked out broken staples. He anesthetized, cleaned, and reinforced his prior incision, covering it with a layer of gauze. "The bleeding's slowing, but he's really tender. I'm requesting a CT scan to make sure everything deep is okay."

Kevin squinted at the officer in the corner who pointedly ignored him. *I'll deal with you later.* He shifted back to his son's battered body. *How can I be angry when you're like this?* He leaned over the side rail, yearning for a connection. "What do you need? What can I do?"

Alex met him with stony silence.

An image of the pig's gaping chest flashed across Kevin's mind. *We were blind and led you straight into the dark.* He pulled back and searched for a place to sit, a weight settling on the base of his skull.

"Susan's on her way. She'll need her head and neck scanned," he said to Steven under his breath.

Steven regarded Alex with apprehension as he stood. "I'll check in on her." He paused mid-step, turning back to Kevin. "Don't leave this time."

The CT tech came shortly thereafter. He slowed upon seeing the officer. "Hi, I'm Duncan. We'll need to remove the handcuffs to transfer him to the CT table."

The officer hesitated, then acquiesced. "Careful, he's violent."

The words cut Kevin. He watched the gurney make its way past, but not before Alex stared at him. The look stopped Kevin cold.

There were only a few moments in Kevin's life where he had felt the gravity of a situation as he was experiencing it. His mother's last smile, Alex's birth, being called 'doctor' for the first time, when he first saw Grace; moments he knew he'd never forget. The look on his son's face had that same importance.

He's saying goodbye.

"Can I come with?!" Kevin blurted.

"Sorry, family has to stay bedside," Duncan said.

"Please."

The tubby tech lifted the head of Alex's bed. "No can do, he'll be back in a few minutes."

Kevin watched them enter an empty hallway. He slowly followed.

"Violent, huh? You seem pretty calm to me," Duncan quipped, pushing Alex from behind. What he couldn't see, was that Alex was surveying the hall ahead of him. He saw a sign for the CT scanner around the corner to the left and the opening double doors of the ambulance bay straight ahead.

Two paramedics entered with a woman on their gurney.

"Stop, that's my mom," Alex said to the startled tech.

"Alex?" Susan's oncoming gurney went still. The paramedic looked at her, guarded. She nodded, reassuring him. They crept forward until she was aligned with her son.

Alex reached over and clutched her hand.

She smiled. "I hope you're okay, honey."

"I don't ..." Words failed him. He closed his eyes and inhaled. *Home.*

Voices around the corner prompted the gurneys to restart. They passed each other and the stillness inside Alex left with her.

How could I do that to you? A shadow slithered into his neck ... spreading.

Just as Alex approached his left turn, an elderly man stepped out. He was hunched over his cane, searching for the cafeteria.

You'll do.

He sprung from the gurney and slammed it back into Duncan, knocking him over.

"Help! What—" The old man's startled objection caught in his throat, as Alex ripped his cane away, causing him to collapse violently.

Alex stepped over his writhing body and rotated to the tech. He brandished the cane above his head. "I fucking dare you."

Kevin clambered around Duncan and the gurney. "Alex, no!" He stopped within feet of his son.

The cane drifted down.

"Do you see what you're doing? This isn't you," he said.

Alex scrutinized his father's panicked face.

Kevin took a step forward and held out his hand.

He gripped the cane tightly and raised it high. Don't!"

Kevin's hand fell, and all hope went along with it.

He watched Alex disappear through the double doors.

Kevin couldn't hear Susan's despondent cries. He couldn't hear the old man scream in pain as he was loaded onto Alex's deserted gurney. All he saw was his boy.

When you first learned how to swim, I've never seen anyone so happy. You were three.

Your blushing pride when you first kissed a girl. You were thirteen.

Your confidence walking off the stage, valedictorian, knowing the job wasn't done yet. Two years ago.

Prized memories … perfect memories … were Kevin's only solace as he went after Alex. He kept up with him into the crowded parking lot, as the jingling keys of the security guards faded behind. Alex was doubled over, snaking around cars quickly and soon fell out of sight, but the startled yelp of a woman steered Kevin back on track. Alex reappeared twenty feet away.

"Please stop. We're your family!" Kevin followed him around a large SUV into a clearing; it was empty. He swiveled, but he couldn't see him anywhere.

He heard shuffling and a blurry figure charged at him. Kevin threw up his hands, but Alex went low.

The cane smashed Kevin's ankle.

"Aghh!"

Kevin collapsed under the blistering pain. He crawled between two cars, scrambling to protect his head from the next blow, but it never came. He looked up at Alex through his fingers. He couldn't see his face; it eclipsed the sun.

"We were wrong, Alex." Kevin winced. "We thought we knew what's best for you."

His fiery silhouette stopped.

"But it's your choice. I can only hope you come back to us."

Alex didn't move ... then he slowly took a step back. He came into focus. All Kevin saw was a man. Resolute.

He pivoted and ran.

Distant shouts. Jingling keys. Louder.

A panting guard came to Kevin and heaved him upright. Kevin pointed at his fleeing son.

The guard peered around the row of cars, tracking Alex. "I can't."

"Why?!"

"He just made it to the street. He's out of my jurisdiction now. Police are on their way."

"It'll be too late." Kevin tested his throbbing ankle. *Fuck!* He gritted his teeth and jogged in agony, making it to the sidewalk. To his horror, Alex took off under the red light of a busy intersection, narrowly missing the edge of a departing city bus. By the time the bus rolled out of frame, Alex was nowhere to be found.

Kevin's compass was gone.

He hobbled down sidewalks, alleyways, but there were no welcoming doors left ajar, no one who could help him. Kevin retraced his painful steps back toward the hospital and watched his world implode.

The guard was waiting with a wheelchair at the edge of the parking lot. Kevin collapsed into it, his swollen ankle feeling as though it were on the verge of tearing through his skin. They found the police officer leaving the ambulance bay. Kevin reluctantly updated him. He was given a card.

He was also given the diagnosis of an ankle fracture, a walking boot, and an ex-wife with a concussion.

They returned to the Atlanta North Hotel in the twilight, battered and exhausted, and, after a sleepless night on their neighboring twin beds, Kevin turned on the local news.

"… the perpetrator of the home invasion is believed to be Alexander Bishop. If you have any information about this man …"

You're alive … and you're being hunted. Please stop running. Stop fighting back. Kevin muted the sound, pulled out the officer's card, and dialed. The police had a warrant, and Alex's suitcase, but no leads, so Kevin and Susan got to work designing notices to photocopy.

That afternoon they clambered into a rental car with stacks of 'Have You Seen Me?' flyers, which yielded nothing but false alarms. They searched block to block to no avail. *How can we find you if we have no idea who you are or what you're capable of?!*

With each passing day the grey crept in, and, after three weeks of scouring Atlanta, Kevin resigned himself to their wretched new reality. *You don't want to be found.*

Susan wouldn't … couldn't accept that. Her wilting exterior contrasted with her steadfast resolve that Alex was nearby. Without a phone or ID, he couldn't have gone far, she reasoned. So, she stayed and reassembled her command station in her new month-to-month rental, armed with four months of income stashed in her savings account. There was nothing left for her in Los Angeles anyway; after weeks of missed deadlines her boss had asked for her resignation.

On his last day in Atlanta, Kevin said goodbye. He hugged Susan over her barren hardwood floor.

"You've always fought so hard for our family, but please, keep yourself strong. For Alex, and for me." Tears flowed for what could have been. "I'm sorry I couldn't fix this."

Informed Consent for Pneuma Transplant

<u>Today we will be assessing whether you:</u>
[X] Understand the transplant process including the procedural details, risks, benefits, and alternatives
[X] Express a choice on whether to proceed consistent with your preferences and values
[X] Appreciate the consequences of participating or refusing
[X] Show appropriate reasoning when comparing these consequences

[X]: Denotes the objective has been completed
[]: Denotes the objective is still pending

This interaction is being video recorded.

———

"There's been a delay."
"I'm so sorry, because of my medical issues?" I ask.
"The other participant never arrived yesterday."
I see him from my window, searching for his card. Forever searching. *Trust this place. It can help you. I can help.*
"Today's a free day." Mr. Montoya's leg shakes again.

"I see. I hope he's okay."

He yields nothing, of course.

I pull out my compact and favorite peach lipstick. "Since we're not in a rush." I reapply, and cringe at the bags under my eyes. *Cut yourself some slack dear, you hardly slept. After all, you thought you'd be dying today.* I snap the compact shut. "I'd like to go outside."

He turns to the observation mirror.

I interrupt him. "Are you always going to follow orders?"

He fights against a flummoxed smile.

"I'm sure you'll catch them up to speed." I push up from the table.

"Please. Can we stay ..." He darts to my side and grabs my rolling oxygen tank.

I ignore his foot-dragging. "Bless your heart." I slide past him; he's pulled along with me. *A new use for my nasal cannula ... a leash!*

I open the door. Cool air tickles my neck.

"Okay ... okay. Just be careful." He guides me through.

We make it to the front steps. He scans our path, before offering his other arm. I take it and we walk down the handicap ramp together. *The wedding I never had.*

It's beautiful out. Just right.

"Where to?" he asks.

I pause to catch my breath. Two handsome Navy men smile as they run by. *So much for my honeymoon.*

"Think you can keep up with them?" he asks.

I blush.

Halfway down the block we sit against a large oak tree. He seems uncomfortable, leaning forward to avoid getting his uniform dirty. I close my eyes and feel every inch of the large roots at my sides. *A perfect chair.*

Then I see her face pressed against the bark.

Out with it.

"We had a tree like this in my backyard." I glance at him, laboring a little for breath.

He's studying me, determining when to call for help.

"Take off your clinical hat. Just listen."

"Sorry."

"One day my friend Helen was over, I think we were eight at the time, and we were being sneaky way up on a branch, throwing acorns at my neighbor's dog. The neighbor complained to my father, and it wasn't my favorite tree anymore. He pushed us against the trunk and used his belt on us. Both of us." My voice cracks.

Keep going.

"I knew what to expect, but the look on her face, she was pleading with me to do something. And I ignored her." I grip the roots. "I remember thinking that Helen, with her perfect family, deserved to know what it felt like at my house. My only friend. I never saw her again. That's when things changed for me. I convinced myself I deserved to be alone." I face my bottled shame head on, feeling the sickening weight of my betrayal. "But it makes you think, was I born cold or did moments like that change my soul too?"

He nods, head down, gracing me with a moment of healing silence. "Life events likely play a role. They usually do. But your transformation after your surgery shows just how much nature's at work here." He allows himself to rest back against the trunk.

We look up at the leaves as a cloud blots out the sun.

"Nature. Isn't it unnerving trying to control it?"

"Terrifying," he says, and smiles that sweet way he does.

A car door opens, shuts.

Dark brown jacket. Black hair.

It's him.

He crosses the street towards our building about fifty feet away, slows, then stops. He turns on the sidewalk and finds me.

He's so young. Oh my god.

That face. That pain. *Helen.*

He lifts his hand slightly before lowering it to his side. It curls into a fist.

I'm a friend. Let me in. All this will end soon.

I slow my inhale and fill with love and gratitude. Through my exhale, I focus on him, wrapping my arms around myself in a warm embrace. I smile.

This is peace, darling one.

27. Cognitive Consonance

Kevin opened the door to his desolate apartment. *So now what? Head back to my shift tomorrow like nothing ever happened?* He stood in the doorway, luggage in hand.

I can't be alone. Not today. The last three weeks were like a lifetime.

He drove to see his father and found him sitting at his kitchen table in his wheelchair, sealing a small white card in an envelope.

Greg folded his hands over it on the table. "Everything hurts."

Kevin reached for the animal crackers. He threw a handful in his mouth and chewed. "How long have you been in pain?"

"Since I've been back."

Weeks. Kevin glanced at Greg's legs: no trauma; no swelling. *I don't think it's your body, Dad.*

Greg slowly leaned back. He stared outside. "Remember when Alex chased Domino? In his Batman underwear?"

Kevin nodded with a fleeting smile. "Inseparable."

Greg's eyes darted around the backyard as if they were still there. He stopped on the fence. "We failed him."

Kevin put the crackers away.

"Had to try something. I couldn't subject him to a lifetime of sitting in his own shit," Greg said.

"We didn't know what we were doing."

"Maybe it's because Alex was changed once before. It's either that, or everyone's 'soul' is set at a different baseline energy level, right?" He tapped his armrest with a growing fervency. "We need a plan. Get everyone back on the same page."

Kevin's pulse quickened. "You're going to experiment on him again?"

Greg glared at his son. "What, you think I'd walk away? Now?"

"I saw him at Valley Green, right before he escaped. He's done, Dad."

"He doesn't know what's going on!"

"Yes, he does. He made it very clear." Kevin took a heavy step forward. "Only his personality changed, right? You talk about Alex and Domino in the backyard, well guess who else has that memory? He knows where we are and how to contact us."

"So, I just sit and wait? Hope he suddenly wants to come home?"

Kevin nodded. "I miss him more than I could ever imagine, and I'm scared of what might happen to him, but we have to let him go. We have to live with that because it's his call, and unless he agrees to it, you're not going to experiment on him again."

"I have to make things right."

"How? Knock him out and throw him on the operating table?"

"Whatever it takes."

"No!" Kevin exploded. "You're trying to control him just like you did with me. Trust me, it'll only add to his resentment."

Greg saw him stare at their photo from the white coat ceremony. He laughed with derision. "I'm so glad we get to revisit your sob story of Dad pushing you to become a successful doctor. One who likes his career, by the way." He unlocked his wheelchair and rolled toward him. "You've had one foot out the door for months and now you finally have your excuse to leave. Pull this crap as soon as it gets difficult."

"This isn't about it being difficult, it's about doing no more harm to him."

"Don't throw medical jargon at me. This is your son. My grandson! It's our responsibility to fix the harm we've already done."

"Not against his will," Kevin pleaded.

"We changed his will. He's this way because of us. We have to keep trying!"

"How? Where do we even begin? Dad, just stop. You're playing God!"

"Doctors play God. That's what we do."

Kevin couldn't hide his disbelief. "What's happened to you?" He moved to the coat rack. "I'm out."

"It's a miracle. You made a decision!" Greg sneered.

The knife turned in Kevin's gut. "Fuck you."

Greg slammed the armrests and pushed himself to his feet. "Watch your mouth! What's happened to me? Look at you. The pigs were your idea, remember? Hell, the case report in the beginning came from you! Then Grace stepped in, and everything changed."

The knife made another revolution. "Leave her out of this."

"She made you soft, weak. You couldn't even function in the backyard. They were just pigs!"

"I told her everything."

Greg recoiled. "What?" He reached for his brow, dropping into his wheelchair.

Kevin advanced. He felt electricity sizzle between his fingers. "You think this is Grace talking? This is finally me. Soft? Weak? If I am, it's because I've always done what you want, trying to please you and protect your precious ego. But I'm done. You're careless and dangerous. You're using my son like a lab rat, just like you used Mom!"

"How dare you!! You betrayed me! You told your little girlfriend and then lied to me. How can we ever trust you?"

"We? You can all go to hell." Kevin grabbed his coat. He walked out of the kitchen and stopped in the foyer. "I lied to protect her."

"From what?"

"You."

Greg's mouth went lax.

"You said it yourself, Dad, you won't stop. Nothing's going to get in your way. But you don't know Grace at all. She loves us. She would never say anything."

Greg wheeled closer. "You knew what was at stake here and you chose your girlfriend over our family."

Kevin's eyes landed on his favorite photo of Linda with Greg's arm draped across her shoulders. "And you chose yourself."

"What the fuck are you talking about? I kept your mother alive. It never compromised us."

Kevin leaned against the wall. He scanned the living room, his old makeshift desk at the dining table, the patio, and slowly straightened up. "For five months you tormented her with useless treatments against her wishes. How'd that work out for us?" He walked to the front door and opened it. As his eyes adjusted to the daylight, he saw Judy on her deathbed, holding her rosary. "Alex has to listen to his inner voice. He can't find it now, but I have faith he will. And if he comes home and wants another procedure, promise me, no more omissions, no more cutting corners. Don't force this, Dad." He faced him, his heart aching as he pulled away. "I love you."

———

Greg sat in silence. Stunned. Broken. *You just ran away like Alex did.*

For the first time in his life, he felt completely abandoned, and not even a knock on the door an hour later would change that.

Greg pulled himself out of the darkness and opened it.

Jasper.

He rolled past him onto the front porch.

Jasper sensed his mood. "Yeah, let's stay out here. It's nice out."

With great difficulty, Greg recounted the argument.

Jasper lowered himself onto the top step. Seemingly claustrophobic, he took off his pullover.

Greg then called Steven and Aaron. He could tell they were relieved to hear of Kevin's departure, but at least they granted him the respect of not flaunting it.

"What are you doing next year, Jasper?" Steven's voice came through Greg's speakerphone.

He took a moment. "Well, Kevin had offered me a job, but in light of recent events I'm not sure. Maybe work part time at a few different—"

"You're still in this?" Steven asked.

Jasper shook his head, biting his lip. He looked at Greg, who gave him a nod. "Yes," Jasper said.

"Something else has come up," Steven said, his voice deeper than normal.

Greg and Jasper exchanged a puzzled look.

"Clarissa, Aaron, and I were suspended from Valley Green indefinitely. Unbeknownst to us, the post-op nurse logged an incident report after Alex punched Aaron. Once administration was involved, the dominoes fell. The anesthesia department protested that while Clarissa was credentialed to perform sedation, it was against hospital policy for her to do it in the OR."

"Wha—" Greg choked on his spit.

Jasper darted to his side, but Greg slammed the armrest, dislodging the offending phlegm. He waved him off.

"Are you okay?" Aaron asked.

"Just a little choking episode. We're good," Jasper said. "Sorry to hear ... wow."

"Yes," Steven said. "Clarissa's out. She plans to move back home to Florida."

And the hits keep fucking coming. Greg wiped his clammy palms on his cuffs. "How was she when you spoke with her?"

His meaning did not escape Steven. "Not great. I'll spare you the details, but she was confrontational. She blamed us for ruining her career and ignoring her religious convictions. Not like it matters. We have her signed non-disclosure agreement."

Jasper rotated back to the street and stared at the driver's seat of his car. He leaned towards it, then stopped.

"Greg, while we're on the topic of non-disclosure agreements, I think it's worth reminding Kevin—"

"He knows," Greg said. "I'd like to think I know my son pretty well. He won't say anything."

"We don't doubt you trust him," Aaron started. "It just seems like it also ended bad—"

"End of discussion. How's your nose by the way?"

"Ha," Aaron scoffed. "Fine."

"We can table this, but it's important," Steven said. "We need to maintain control before we expand."

"Expand?" Jasper asked.

"Well, we don't have a facility anymore, so I approached my sister Diane—"

"What?!" Greg and Jasper exclaimed.

"Unless I'm missing something, we don't have other options."

"Wait, your sister, the senator?" Greg asked.

"Yes."

"How much did you tell her?"

"I just told her what we need ... a clean OR ... surgical instruments. She reached out to a colleague, Lawrence

Kedge, and they found one. Ford Hospital. It's in a Navy base in Chicago."

"Holy shit," Greg said. *It must be that massive one on the northside.*

"I say we act on this, but you get the final call, Greg. This is for Alex."

He mulled it over. "You'd both stay on board?"

"Of course," Steven said.

Greg leaned on his elbows. "What do they want in return?"

"Unclear. We can flesh out the details later."

"Alex is a time bomb. A Navy base would offer manpower," Aaron said.

Greg received an optimistic nod from Jasper.

"What's your working diagnosis?" Greg asked.

"He's manipulative and has no insight, exhibits violent tendencies, of course, but it's too early to tell."

"You need time with him," Jasper said. "But nobody knows where he is and even if we find him, he hates us. We may have to expand on that front and—"

"Before we get ahead of ourselves," Steven interjected, to Jasper's noticeable frustration, "can we agree to at least secure this facility? Diane's family, and I'd like to think I know her pretty well."

Greg smirked. "Sure, you do." *Politicians can always be trusted. But this could work ... another chance. And this time, I'll get it right: the right questions, with the right science behind it.* He owed that to Alex. And Kevin. "Okay."

"Here we go," Jasper mouthed. He signaled he was thirsty.

"Guys, we'll be right back." Greg hit mute. "Grab me a water?"

They headed inside through the front door as Greg's wheels slowed on the living room carpet.

Then Greg's senses split.

He heard excited screams coming from his neighbor's yard. Springtime joy, like the squeals of ... *pigs.* His eyes widened, then tracked out the window, down the steps, onto the backyard grass. *Where he saw Jasper and Kevin, back-to-back, rotating in unison, cradling two 'souls.'*

Oh my god.

Before Greg could speak, Jasper's sprint-walk barreled down on him. He hit unmute on the phone. "I've got something to say, and Steven, you better let me talk this time."

Greg looked at him with knowing excitement.

"Soul transplant."

28. ALL CAPS

Grace waved goodbye to the valet Carl as she crossed the drop-off loop of Saint Monica Hospital. Her other hand was in her purse, unfolding the small blade hidden within one of her keys. She wasn't taking any chances after a colleague was recently carjacked.

She entered the shadowy parking lot, struggling to shake the feeling that the recent uptick in crime reflected a bigger issue. Medicine was losing its humanity. Desperate patients were being thrown out of the hospital prematurely and Grace's objections were falling on deaf ears. *We've become cogs in a broken corporate mach—*

She stopped. There was a man on her bumper.

And there was no one around.

She pulled out the key knife. *Ready.*

The man saw her and came closer.

Kevin.

She stopped breathing.

His smile was reserved but his eyes were accessible, vulnerable.

She sheathed her weapon.

His hand slid to his abdomen. "I'm still having that pain. Think I should check in?" He cocked his head to the side.

Grace turned a shade of crimson in the darkness. "It's probably gas." She curled her hair behind her ear and looked down. Her brow furrowed as she saw his walking boot.

"Alex broke my ankle."

Grace pulled back, concerned. "You went through with it. You operated on him."

"And turned him into something worse."

Dormant emotions surfaced inside her. She could only shake her head.

They slowly made their way back to her car.

"I went to my mom's tree and sat for hours," Kevin said. "My head was finally clear, and I felt you."

She turned away. "Kevin, I ..."

"All I could hear was what you said on the rooftop. Grace, I tried to explain to Alex what was wrong with him. Help him understand what we were planning to do, but they rushed his surgery and now he's full of rage. He lashed out at us and disappeared, and we can't find him." Kevin fought back tears, tortured by grief. He leaned back on the car for support. "We've only added to his suffering, and I can't do it anymore. I'm done."

She lowered her purse to the ground and joined him. "What'll you do if he comes home?"

"I'll be his father."

Grace's shield cracked. "I hope you're not doing this because of me. I didn't ask—"

"It's for me."

Their eyes met.

"With every step in this process, the brutal experiments, the deception, I lost part of me too. I pushed on with the obsession that we could restore Alex, but nothing was worse than seeing his disintegration and knowing I helped create it. So, I left. It destroyed my relationship with Dad, but now I finally respect myself again. I've decided the most loving thing I can do is to let Alex live his life and make his own decisions. Even though he chose to push us away."

Grace received his words with care. "Is Alex capable of making his own decisions now?"

"Yes. I think so. They're just ones I wish he wouldn't make."

She nodded.

"But I'm learning from this." Kevin stood. "And with more time alone I hope I'll grow even more. There's just one problem with that."

Grace gazed up at him.

"I don't want to do this without you. I'm deeply in love with you."

She hesitated, as the pain of their final week together crept in. *You left me alone and so confus—*

"I wish I could change what I did to us, but I promise I'll strive to be the best version of myself. You deserve nothing less."

Her head dipped slightly, as she absorbed the gentle moment. The caution and fear left.

"I will protect this." Kevin offered his hands to her.

Grace slid her palms onto his.

Kevin eased her close and she rested her head on his shoulder.

Thank you. He held her tight. "Can I take you somewhere? Anywhere?"

She paused, before taking a step back. Melancholy drifted between them. "I'm sorry about Judy too. She was remarkable in so many ways, and I know she was a lifeline for you," Grace said.

"Yes, she was. I'm glad you had time together."

"She told me what happened with you and James."

Kevin collapsed inward. "After we broke up, I shut down. I couldn't tell him anything."

"And I lied to him to protect your secret." She turned a shade of crimson, this time, he suspected, for another reason.

He felt the full depth of her frustration. "I hate that I put you in that situation," Kevin said. "I can't tell you how sorry I am."

"James is one of the best people I know. He's loyal, righteous, and don't you think he's worth the price of a non-disclosure agreement?"

Kevin's head fell. He was back on the lakefill, watching James walk away. *How could I let a piece of paper do so much damage?*

"We should see him together," she said.

"Together," Kevin agreed. Grace wasn't the only one he had felt at his mom's tree. *My team.* "Mind if I drive?"

"Wait ... now?"

"Yes." He walked to the passenger door, opening it for her.

Kevin watched her settle in and then maneuvered behind the wheel, taking her keys. "I just need to stop by my car to grab something."

Fifteen minutes later, they parked outside *The Nightcap.*

"I felt like I'd known her for years," Grace said. "Always warm and supportive."

"That's Judy." He shut off the engine and nervously tapped the armrest.

Grace slid her hand over his. "Game plan?"

"Just the truth."

"All of it?"

"Yeah."

They exited the car and headed towards the glow. Flowers lined the entrance of the brick building. Kevin's eye was caught by a pristine purple orchid, towering above its wilted neighbors. *That's Judy.*

He reached for the door. "After you."

She stopped. "He should see you first."

An icy pulse locked his hand. A familiar panic set in. *What if he never talks to me again? Will this only make things worse?* Kevin's mind reeled, but he wrenched himself back into the present and breathed through it ... and around it. He opened the door.

"We're clos—" James stopped halfway through drying a glass. His eyes landed on each of them; happiness flickered, but it was quickly stamped out. He slowly turned and placed the glass behind him with a malicious smile. The one you get right before a punch to the face.

Just one witness left.

"Alright Frank, gotta get you moving buddy," James said.

"How come they get to stay?" The old man whined, grabbing his coat. He shuffled to a large cross on the wall with *Angel of Mundelein* above it. "Goodnight, Judy."

James led him to the door and locked eyes with Kevin. "They'll be right behind you. See you tomorrow."

The door shut; the hanging bell jingled; he muffled it. Brushing past them, James returned to the bar. "How's the new boyfriend, Grace? What's his name again?"

She reached for Kevin's hand.

James smelled blood. He smiled. "Did you even give him a name?"

"C'mon James," Kevin said.

"I'll get to you next," he snipped.

"She doesn't deserve that," Kevin said. "This is all on me."

"Of course, it is."

"I'm sorry, James," Kevin said.

James shrugged impassively. He picked up the glass and resumed drying it. "Anything else I can help you with?"

"Permission to approach the bench."

He studied him, before glancing at Grace. "You can sit."

She left Kevin's side and settled onto a stool. Kevin cautiously approached and stood next to her.

James raised his arm to the shelf behind him. "Pick your poison."

"Tequila," Kevin said.

"Now I know you're full of shit." He grabbed the murky bottle off the bottom shelf.

Kevin's eyes widened as the lumpy, dark liquid flowed out. "If this is what it takes, so be it." He reached for the shot of sludge. "Can we go to the back room?"

"Why would we go back there? Here's fine," James said.

"Pour me one," Grace said. "If we're punishing ourselves, count me in. I'm sorry too."

James's teeth clenched. He reached for another glass and stopped. "What's going on here?" His hand trembled.

"I'll explain," Kevin said. "Just please, better tequila."

James pulled his hand back and slipped it inside his pocket. He chuckled. "I can't believe both of you were going to drink that. That's so fucked."

Grace snorted; she covered her laugh.

James's eyes rolled. He grabbed a new bottle and poured two shots. He watched them gulp it down, taking some delight in their struggle, before pounding the bar top. "My bar, my rules. We do this my way. Back room, Grace." He turned to Kevin. "Bottom shelf only. Don't burn the place down."

They disappeared behind the curtain. Kevin walked around the bar and opened the office door. He reached into his coat, pulled out James's baseball glove, and placed it on his chair.

On top of the desk was a pamphlet for Sunnyville nursing home.

Margaret.

As close as he was to James, he hardly knew his mother. She was always there, but in the background. Small in frame and personality, she was the type where you'd fear a loud noise would shatter her. James's Dad often did. When he died her mind went with him.

Kevin returned to the bar and poured himself a glass of red label. He sat and caught his reflection. *Get through this. Heal it.*

He heard the curtain part. One set of footsteps. Dress pants took the chair next to him.

Kevin didn't move.

"When did the lies start?" James's voice was measured.

"When I came back from Atlanta. Lied to her too."

"Why did you need the pigs?"

"When Dad tried to save Alex, he accidentally changed his 'soul.' That's why he woke up different, we just didn't know it at the time. We used the pigs to simulate Alex and experiment on the 'soul' again, and Grace walked in on it. I told her everything and once she heard our plan, she broke up with me."

James left his stool. He walked around the bar and poured a glass. He took the shot. "Keep going."

"We were legally bound not to say anything. Deep down I knew it was all fucked up. I didn't want to bring you into this mess, but I should've told you. And it only got worse. We changed Alex again and it blew up in our faces. Now he's on a rampage. Took off on his own."

"This story is literally too fucking crazy for you both to make up."

Kevin took a swig.

"Where did you last see Alex?" James asked.

"Atlanta."

"Can I come out?" Grace peeked from behind the curtain.

James looked at Kevin. "We'll come to you."

They migrated through the curtain and sat. James went to close the back door.

"What do you think you're doing, Dowd?"

"Don't worry, I'm keeping the traditions. It's closing time."

Kevin summoned him back. "Not yet."

James grinned and returned to the table. "So, what happens next?"

"They'll try to find Alex and do it all over again," Kevin said.

"And you're out?"

"Out."

"Probably the right call. What a clusterfuck." The tension returned to James's shoulders, his face knotting with concern. "Alex isn't just a threat to himself, he's a danger to everyone."

Air left the room.

"Hey." James clinked Kevin's glass. "Want me to find him?"

"I have to step back from this," Kevin said.

"I don't."

Test Subject 2
Interaction 10
Ford Hospital
071000SMAY19

Informed Consent for Pneuma Transplant

<u>Today we will be assessing whether you:</u>
[X] Understand the transplant process including the procedural details, risks, benefits, and alternatives
[X] Express a choice on whether to proceed consistent with your preferences and values
[X] Appreciate the consequences of participating or refusing
[X] Show appropriate reasoning when comparing these consequences

[X]: Denotes the objective has been completed
[]: Denotes the objective is still pending

This interaction is being video recorded.

———

I made those bastards see what it feels like to be given hope, only to be forced to wait. *Makes you want to tear your hair out, doesn't it?* I would've stayed away again, but I can't get my parents out of my head. *They're everywhere, lifeless, and they're even closer when I shut my eyes.*
I had to come back here.

I feel that same pull now. It turns me around.

A sick old woman is sitting against a tree, looking right at me.

Do I know you? What the fuck. Why are you staring at me?

She hugs herself and her face lights up with a smile.

Why are you reaching out to me?

And then it hits me. *It's you. You're showing me my future.*

A feeling I don't understand overwhelms me. *I need to get inside.*

I enter the hall and drop into the nearest chair, waiting for my balance to return. Lowry stands guard outside of the interview room. He mutters into his radio.

As I approach the door, he holds his hand up.

"Not today," I say. "Move."

He doesn't.

"Or am I going to have to move you?" I jab two fingers into his chest. "Always a pain in my ass."

A voice comes through his radio with a crackle. "Ready. Let him in."

Lowry steps aside and opens the door. Mom's perfume hits me again. *Fuck, I can't take this any ...*

Grandpa's sitting at the table.

That saggy fuck finally came out to say hi. I glare at his nauseating neck fat billowing over his collar like a mushroom.

"Hi Alex." He silently waits for my move.

Keep waiting then.

"I'm sorry," Greg says.

"Yes. You are."

"Please sit with me."

Hell no. "Have you been behind the mirror the whole time? Hiding behind those senators and Navy meatheads?"

"I've been with you every step. We were afraid that if you saw me, it would trigger you and end this before it started, but family seems to be the only way to reach you."

"Oh yeah, your perfume trick."

"You have every reason not to trust this process and every right to hate all of it. I've failed you and—"

"Repeatedly."

He grimaces.

"Not to mention calling the cops on me in Atlanta over two wallets."

"Alex, that wasn't me." Greg leans forward. "The gift shop owner called it in. You were on security cam—"

"Stop lying to me!"

"I've never lied to you. Never!"

"You just have others do it for you."

Greg falls back into his chair. His eyes break away.

"I'm so sick of being under your thumb. Never again. I'm in control," I say.

He holds up his hands helplessly. "You've always been in control. All of this is for you. Nothing matters to me here, but you."

"Your words mean nothing. You promised you'd 'make things right' but all you've done is hurt me."

"Then if all this doesn't work, you get to hurt me. You want to take your life? Take mine first. I'm in this with you until the end."

My parents appear behind him. Everyone's here ... for me.

"You held onto my card for a reason. I believe you still have hope," Greg says.

I close my eyes. "I lost it."

He reaches into his coat. "This is for you, then." He places a pocket watch on the table.

It can't be.

"I keep it with me every day."

I hold it in my palm. It's perfect. Just like when I returned it to him when I was a boy, except the two black hands are frozen. I turn it over and find an etching I had forgotten:

YOU ONLY HAVE SO MUCH
TIME WITH HIM

MAKE IT COUNT

"Alex, let's go home."

29. CULMINATION

"You'd better have a breath mint before you see Alex. You know he hates smoking!" Kevin calls to Susan from across the street.

No sooner does he step off the curb than a blurry figure nearly crashes into him.

"Sorry!" The Navy recruit bellows over his shoulder, continuing his sprint. "More coming!"

A herd of blue sweatsuits gallop past. After what seems like minutes, Kevin tests a gap in the action and jumps back again, dodging a straggler.

He blinks at Susan.

She takes a drag.

He joins her and they stare up at the decommissioned hospital. Ivy scales the stone walls, brazenly creeping into the windows.

"Are you okay?" he asks. "Atlanta was brutal for you."

"I'm alive," she says. "So, I guess old Navy hospitals are just as shitty as old civilian ones."

"I guess so." Kevin smiles. "I'm glad you're here. We need you with us."

"God, do you think it'll work this time? Are they ready? Alex can't go through this anymore. He just can't!"

"I'm hopeful."

Kevin drapes his arm around her, squeezing her shoulder. "They're all on board with this new approach and I'm grateful Alex consented to it."

He motions her toward the entrance, but she doesn't move.

She takes another drag.

He's captivated by the glowing ember of her cigarette. "I've forgotten how good that smells. Give me a hit, okay?"

The calming smoke fills his lungs.

They hear footsteps behind them. Grace.

Kevin coughs, quickly giving the cigarette back to Susan. He steps away from her.

Without breaking stride, Grace extends her hand. "Hi Susan, I'm Grace. Glad to meet you."

They shake hands. "Nice to meet you too."

"I'm sorry it's such a stressful time."

Susan nods, extinguishing her cigarette. "I hear you're friends with James?"

"My brother trained with him in San Diego. I'm from there."

"Ah, military family." Susan glances at Kevin, surprised.

Grace's eyes narrow slightly. "Just Brody and me."

Susan steals a look at Grace's toned arms and slips her bandaged fingers into her pockets. "You must feel right at home here. Is your family still in San Diego?"

"My parents."

"And Brody?"

Kevin sees Grace's chest twist.

"He died, years ago," Grace said.

"Oh. I'm so sorry."

"It's okay. You didn't know."

"Brody was with James in Afghanistan. It happened while saving a family caught in a crossfire," Kevin says.

Grace notices Susan biting her chapped lip. She hands her a bottle of water from her purse.

Susan pauses, before accepting the offering. "Thanks. Your brother and James are heroes. James found Alex in three days. He did what I couldn't in four weeks. I don't know how he does it, but he always steps up."

Kevin shares a smile with Grace. "He's the only one that could reach Alex in this state."

"I'm glad they're under the same roof now," Susan says. "It was great to see James in Atlanta. I cooked him dinner his first night there. I'm glad he was eating, he looked thin, at least by his standards."

"He's had a rough year," Kevin says.

"How come he's not here?"

Kevin feels Grace shift next to him. "I don't think this is the best environment for James. He's taking a break from Navy stuff," he says.

"Oh, he didn't mention that. Well, please tell him thank you again for bringing our boy back," Susan says.

"You'll get your chance to tell him tomorrow night. He said he'd meet us back at Dad's."

"That'd be nice."

They start for the steps and pass through the front entrance which has been left ajar. A guard acknowledges them with a nod. Three folding chairs wait for them in the drafty main hall.

Kevin's phone buzzes. A text from Jasper fills the screen:

We're starting

Jasper is floors above them, pushing a gurney with Katherine Trudy on it. They turn a corner, and a row of empty operating rooms stretch ahead of them.

She feels sunlight hit her cheek. *This is it.* "Dr. Richardson, can you stop here a moment?"

"Of course." Jasper watches her take in the view. He slides her closer to the window. "I'll be around the corner. Just holler when you're ready."

Katherine marvels at the city of her dreams. *If only I could've restarted here, the way I am now.*

Fantasies of a parallel life unfurl. Living in a Chicago high rise, befriending the local baker, bumping into the man of her dreams on a corner. Then, she sees her father as a young boy, playing in the street with his friends. He's happy and full of light. He's free.

The last thing I see.

Katherine smiles and closes her eyes. "Okay."

She feels movement beneath her. A click on the wall, then a door opens. The sound narrows.

She's in the OR.

Her bed rotates and stops.

Someone holds her hand. "Thank you," he says.

Then another person. "Knowing you has been one of the biggest pleasures of my life. Thank you."

That's Dr. Ikahashi. Her lip trembles. She wipes away a tear.

The door opens again, and the room goes quiet.

A gurney stops next to her.

"Doing okay, Alex?" Dr. Ikahashi asks.

"Yes," he says, near her feet.

Katherine swells. *Alex.* That's his na—"

"I knew it was you by the tree."

She opens her eyes and gazes into his. "Alex, I'm Katherine. I hope you know nothing but happiness, dear."

He stays on her face, unable to find the words, as he's helped onto a sterile, padded table.

She closes her eyes again. She scans the rooftops behind her eyelids. She's floating above the Chicago River. She follows it to the lake. *What an adorable little park by the water.*

Grass rises to her feet. Katherine approaches a table to find she's already seated there, across from Beatrice, playing chess.

Sleep enters her veins.

———

The room comes into focus around Greg, Steven, and Jasper.

"Defibrillators are on, both set at fifty joules of monophasic energy," Greg says. He acknowledges a guest in the corner, standing in ill-fitting scrubs. "Senator Kedge is here to observe. Thank you again for this facility. Can you see from where you are?"

"Call me Lawrence. I can see fine." He adjusts his mask.

"Do you have any questions about the non-disclosure agreement you signed?"

"I do not."

Greg takes a deep breath, studying the two patients head-to-toe in front of him. "Any questions?"

"Let's make history." Steven says, as Jasper grabs the iodine.

Blades, scissors, rib spreaders, open.

A ball forms in Lawrence's throat; he fights the urge to turn away. Then it happens. Two blue lights illuminate his wide eyes. Steven removes Katherine's light and transfers it inside Alex's chest while Jasper simultaneously removes Alex's and separates his hands; Alex's blue light disappears into thin air.

Brimming with new energy, they monitor Alex closely. Steven goes to work repairing his chest.

"That's it? That fast?" Lawrence exclaims.

"That's it," Greg says. "The hard part is waiting to see what happens after the sedation wears off."

"That was truly astounding. Thank you all." Lawrence slides along the wall, avoiding the surgical stands. "I look forward to hearing about Alex. Steven, keep me posted?"

Steven nods.

Lawrence glances at Katherine's monitor before he exits: her numbers are all zero, flashing silently.

He finds Diane Dreucetti in the hallway, leaning against the wall in a red blazer.

"How was it?" she asks.

"Astonishing. Extraordinary. I'm still searching for the right words." Lawrence takes off his mask and surgical cap. His attention is drawn to the Chicago skyline over her shoulder. He gazes beyond it. *Revolutionary.* "I'm surprised you didn't want to watch."

"I don't like blood," she says. "I'm sure I'll hear the highlights from Steven at dinner. Join us?"

Lawrence glances at his watch. "I'll let you catch up with your brother. Let's enjoy family time while we can. My son's almost here. Thank you though." He tears off his disposable yellow gown and dumps it in the nearest trash can. "What will they do with her body?"

"Cremation and dispersal. Montoya's already outside."

He nods. "I guess that's it, then. I still can't believe what I just saw."

"What a week. I'll see you back in Washington." She stops midturn. "Do I have your vote on the pipeline?"

"Yes."

She smiles. "Safe flight."

Greg soon emerges through the same door, pushing Alex on his gurney. They make their slow trek to the recovery room, where Sally receives them.

"Transporting him yourself, huh? Isn't that what residents are for?" Sally nudges him.

"Jasper's past hazing at this point," he says through heavy breaths.

"Get some rest, old man. There's a cot one room over. I'll come a-knocking when he's awake."

Greg shakes his head. "I don't want Alex out of my sight. Besides, I don't sleep much anymore." He sits by the window, looking out from his perch. *Please no more hospitals. Please let this be it.*

There's chatter below. He sees Lawrence, now in his Navy uniform, walking down the steps towards an idling black SUV. The driver helps him enter, closes Lawrence's door, and circles the hood. He's dressed similarly, young, with Lawrence's face. They drive off to the salute of gate guards.

Greg looks at his hands, the same hands that let his control slip away.

"You've kept me sidelined for a while now. You know that's gonna cost ya." Sally places a blanket on Alex.

"I'll pay it forward. Thanks again."

"I'm not just talking about Alex. Have you talked to Kevin?"

"He's downstairs."

"And?"

Greg returns to Alex's monitor.

She shakes her head. "I'll be right back with the morphine."

Morphine. Greg's in a fog, as if he's already received some; a dream state comprising most of his days, not truly asleep or awake. Mostly numb. *Purgatory.*

The familiar squeaks of her sneakers return, and she leaves him be. They coexist, waiting for—

"Grandpa?"

Greg's eyes quickly refocus. Alex is looking at him.

"The procedure's over, you're okay," Greg says.

"How's my warrior?" Sally comes closer.

"Sally? Oh … wow. Hi," he slurs, winces.

"Let's get you feeling better." She gives him the dose. She gently holds his arm, as he settles into his opiate glow.

"I just had the craziest dream," Alex says. "I was back in the ocean."

"Nice dream?" she asks.

He smiles. "Yes."

Sally nods at the bedside table. "Something's waiting for you. I was told it's from Katherine Trudy."

Alex looks at them, confused.

Greg sees the propped envelope and picks it up. "The other participant."

"Katherine," Alex mouths, before the tears come. "I can't believe she did all this for me."

"Want me to open it?"

"Yes," Alex says to his grandfather.

Greg opens it and gasps. He pulls out his small white card, struggling to speak. "I will make things right ..." Unable to go on, he hands it to Alex.

"I promise." Alex finishes it for him. "It's your card, Grandpa! She found it." He clutches it tightly, slowly lowering it into his lap. "And you kept your promise. Thank you."

"I did?" The mountain shakes.

———

Alex closes his eyes. He can feel waves now. *Just like in my dream.* But there's sand under his feet. The sand turns to soil, then soft grass, extending as far as he can see. He's under the shining sun and takes in the warmth. *Yes.*

30. REUNION

The elevator doors open. Across the hallway, he's the first thing they see.

They hold Alex's gaze. He taps the side rail of his bed. Greg lowers it and retreats to the bench by the window, as Alex fights against the pain and tries to stand.

They rush into the room, and Kevin wraps his arms around Alex, easing him back down.

Alex exhales through quivering lips, clutching his father. He sees the walking boot. Shame and dismay streak down his cheeks. "I'm so sorry."

"You don't ever have to apologize." Kevin sits on the bed next to him. "How do you feel?"

Alex manages a nod before he settles onto his father's shoulder, sniffling. "I love you, Dad."

"Aww, my boy."

Rays begin to emerge from Kevin's charcoal core. He hesitates. *I was deceived before. What if I lose him again?* He acknowledges the intrusive thoughts and lets them pass, embracing the moment. "I love you too. So much."

Susan glides in and leans over her son. Tears of relief shine in her eyes.

Alex reaches for her, stopping halfway. "Are you ..."

She leads his hand to her face and nestles it. "I'm okay."

Kevin relaxes into the joy of their reunion and turns to see Greg across the room, studying Alex. *He's on the outside, looking in.*

He joins him and lowers his hand softly onto Greg's scarred knee. "Thank you."

Greg pats his son's hand, before his arms fold across his chest. He returns to Alex's profile.

Kevin follows his stare. "Want to come outside, get some air?"

Greg takes in a ragged breath, almost as if he's forgotten how to do it. He doesn't even notice Aaron enter the room. "I want to be here for Aaron's evaluation. He's on his way."

Kevin glances at his father with mounting concern. "Can I stay here with you?"

Greg nods.

Aaron assesses Alex for an hour with everyone present. He closes a folder with a sigh and hands him his business card. "Everything's looking good, Alex. I'll give you a call tomorrow, but feel free to reach out anytime, okay? It's really nice to meet you. I'm impressed by your resilience, and your right hook."

Susan laughs, as Alex grins sheepishly.

Steven and Jasper appear in the doorway.

"Looks like some fun in here," Jasper says.

"All done." Aaron stands.

"Thank you very much, Alex," Steven says. "This has been a grueling process for you, and you have been very heroic. No words can fully express our gratitude."

Alex smiles. "I'm not sure I deserve all that praise. I caused so much trouble but thank you."

"There was a learning curve for us all. We just want you to know we'll always be close as your team. I hope we keep in touch."

"I'd like that."

"Can I steal your family for a moment?" Steven asks.

Alex nods.

Kevin helps Greg to his feet, and they join the small circle in the hallway.

"He seems thoughtful, reflective," Aaron says. "I didn't see any red flags at all."

"I didn't either, but it's hard to tell so soon, right?" Susan picks her finger and catches herself, jerking her arms to her sides.

Aaron taps his nose. "I have a pretty good sense for these things."

"Really?!"

Aaron beams. "I think we did it."

Susan springs forward, hugging Aaron and Steven.

Momentarily bewildered, they awkwardly reciprocate.

"Thank you for saving Alex," she says, "and our family."

Kevin nods in agreement, addressing them. "And thank you for your persistence, even when I pushed back."

Handshakes ensue.

"Glad to hear your nose still works," Jasper says to Aaron.

Steven stands tall. "This is it for us. It's been a journey. Thank you for your leadership on this, Greg. You've exceeded your reputation."

"Everyone did well against all odds. Thank you," Greg says.

———

The Atlanta team heads for the elevator, signaling Jasper, who jogs to catch up.

"I've underestimated you," Steven says.

Jasper slows. "Thanks?"

"We've been granted access to this facility for the foreseeable future. We can do a lot of good here. What do you think?"

Jasper's feet fuse with the tile. "I ... don't know. It ... it's fulfilling. I just don't know how much pro bono work I can keep doing. I have loans and I'm just starting—"

"If money and loans were no longer an issue, what would you say?"

He stares at them, trying to regain equilibrium. "I'd strongly consider it."

"I may hold you to that." Steven presses the elevator call button. "We'd, of course, love Greg's involvement too, but we know how hard this week's been on him."

"I'll see what I can do." Jasper peers down the hall at his mentor. When he turns back, the elevator doors are closing on Steven and Aaron. They're smiling.

Kevin is next to go downstairs. He finds Grace in the lobby, bent forward, engrossed with her phone. She sees him and quickly tucks it away along with a remnant of consternation.

"Tell me, tell me." She stands.

"I think he's going to be okay!" Kevin hugs her, lifting her off her feet. "He told me he loved me."

"Oh! That's amazing! I'm so happy for you all. Is everyone on cloud nine?"

"Getting there."

"I mean, that's totally understandable. This is so exciting. I can't wait to meet him!"

"Me too. Wan—" Kevin sees a flash of red from the corner of his eye. It's a woman in a red blazer. She's outside, walking away with Steven and Aaron. "Who's that?"

"I'm not sure, but there's something I—"

"Kevin," Susan calls out from the elevator, holding the door open. "Sorry for interrupting, but Alex is asking for you."

Grace kisses Kevin on the cheek. "Go. I'll see you tomorrow."

"Come up with me," Kevin says to Grace.

"Tomorrow. Today's for family," Grace says.

"Are you sure?" Kevin asks.

She smiles, nods.

"I'm so glad you came."

Kevin joins Susan and they head back upstairs. They step into a hallway filled with music.

"The radio by his bed has Bluetooth. He's been creating a playlist," Susan says.

Kevin's back in his garage, teaching Alex chord progressions on his guitar.
Our own little world. Let's go back soon.

They near the room and Greg steps out, sliding into a seat in the hall. He's gripping his shirt, balling it into his closed fist.

"Dad, what's wrong?" Kevin crouches next to him. "I'll meet you in there, Susan."

She steps inside.

Greg rocks in place. "Alex looks okay. Why can't I ... I want to feel relief, but I can't ... I can't."

"You've been through trauma. You've buried so much."

"And it's been too long." Greg starts searching for the exits. "I have to get out of here."

"C'mon Dad, breathe." Kevin lays his hand over Greg's fist, gently pressing it into his chest. He feels it loosen. "When you bury pain, it doesn't decompose. You have to feel it. It's the only way to find relief." Kevin rises in front of him. "You don't have to keep fighting anymore. It's over, Dad."

Greg's face contorts, turning purple, before unleashing a torrent of tears. He lowers his head, sobbing.

Kevin holds him. Then, the opening bars of 'Hotel California' reach his ears from his son's room.

31. AFTER

Kevin watches the last guard close the entrance to the hospital and lock it. He twirls his keys and heads down the steps.

"Thanks Lowry!"

The guard flinches and looks at Alex. His face goes flat.

Alex gives him a warm nod from the backseat of Kevin's SUV. "Thanks for keeping us safe."

Lowry's puzzlement slowly morphs into a smile. He waves goodbye.

Kevin pulls out of the Navy base. He tries to focus on the road, but he can't help but look back in his rear view at Alex. His hand is out of the window, surfing the breeze.

Enjoy the moment, my son. Enjoy everything.

They turn a bend and Lake Michigan appears on their right. The gothic towers of Kevin's alma mater come into view in the distance.

"There's something about this city," Alex says.

Kevin does a double take in the mirror. "Yeah?"

Alex nods enthusiastically.

"I never left for a reason," Greg says from the passenger seat.

Kevin straightens, about to burst. "We love it here and there are some great medical schools. Just saying."

"Medical school," Alex slowly enunciates the words. He looks back outside.

Kevin taps the wheel, trying to recalibrate to Alex's new wavelength. His eyes reluctantly return to the highway.

"What should I cook today?" Greg asks.

"Whatever you want, Grandpa. Just please, no more fast food."

"Maybe I'll save burgers for another day then."

Kevin glances at Greg's gut. "Maybe another month."

"Hey." Greg jabs his arm. "You're a Midwesterner again. We eat meat here. Please tell me LA didn't turn you into a health nut."

Kevin pokes back. "Quantity, Dad."

They arrive at Greg's house thirty minutes later. Kevin helps Alex disembark and they stand shoulder to shoulder. Kevin gently squeezes his arm. "Welcome back."

Alex beams. He wanders onto the front lawn, admiring his sneakers, as they glide through the overgrown grass. "It's such a nice day, I'd like to stay outside."

"Sounds good." Kevin basks in his light. *He's finally at peace ... in a field of green.* "Meet you out back?"

"Yeah."

"I can't believe you're here. Everyone's on their way. I'm excited for you to meet Grace."

"Me too."

Kevin turns to see Greg clamber up the steps, gripping the wooden rail tightly. He catches up to him and supports his final ascent, leading him through the front door. Greg opts to rest in the wheelchair. Kevin grabs the ukulele and joins Alex in the backyard.

They stop at the pile of lumber. "Remember our summer project?"

Alex nudges a haphazard plank with his foot. "Wow. Yes."

"Wish we had time to finish it before you leave."

"I'm sure we'll find something else to do." Alex takes the ukulele from him. "This is more my pace." He lowers himself to the ground and sits cross-legged, tuning it, as the rest of the party trickles in.

Grace is the last to enter and warmly greets Alex.

He tries to stand, but she waves him back down and joins him.

"Please rest. I love hanging out on the grass," Grace says. "That ukulele is so cool."

Alex holds it out, showing her the detailed woodwork. "Isn't it? I can show you a few chords if you're interested."

Their animated back and forth draws smiles all around.

Kevin looks at each carefree face. Jasper, head held high, has new grey hair sprouting near his temples. Confidence restored; his training is complete. Susan, arms resting comfortably at her sides, has new color and vitality. Her light is breaking through. Greg, earnestly looking back at Kevin, nods, and places his hand over his own heart. A thank you, but more importantly, it's an understanding.

Reunited at last. We made it.

Grace is engrossed in Alex's finger positions on the frets, as Susan walks up and drops to a knee next to her son.

"I could really use a hug."

"Oh, Mom." Alex hands Grace the ukulele and embraces his mother. They hold each other with gentle ease. Susan rocks him softly, kissing his forehead. "And I may need a few more."

"Absolutely," Alex says.

Susan stands, exchanging a kind nod with Grace, before walking past Kevin. She gives him a look, *don't fuck it up,* and makes her way to the kitchen with Jasper to prep the chicken. Greg assumes his time-honored tradition manning the grill.

Kevin mouths the word 'James' to Grace.

She shakes her head. "Phone," she mouths back, before refocusing on her conversation with Alex.

Kevin pulls out his cell and sees an unread text from her:

James isn't home and he's not returning my texts. I'm on my way. Be there in 15

Kevin double-checks his missed calls. Nothing.

She comes to his side, turning more pensive by the second. "You haven't heard from him either?"

"No. He wouldn't miss something like this."

Kevin calls and it goes straight to voicemail. He shoots James a text and immediately receives an alert that it's not delivered.

"What the fuck," Kevin says under his breath. "I've gotta go make sure he's okay."

"I'm coming with," Grace says.

Alex sees his father's concern and signals him for help up. They quickly congregate at the grill.

"Dad ..." Kevin starts.

Greg shakes the empty bottle of lighter fluid and tosses it aside in disgust.

"Can we push dinner an hour? We have to go help a friend. Sorry, it's really important."

"Everything okay?"

"Hope so. We'll grab lighter fluid on the way back."

He nods. "It's getting dark. Don't take too long."

"Greg, we need you in here!" Susan's calls out.

He leaves his lit cigarette on the grill stand and plods through the twilight towards the kitchen.

Alex moves closer to his father. "Is there anything I can do?"

"I think we've got it under control, but thanks for asking," Kevin says. "Want us to get you some dessert?"

"No thanks."

"See you in a bit." They start through the side gate. Before the door shuts, Kevin looks back at Alex.

His face is glowing. He's taking a drag.

Grace reaches for Kevin's hand, but he doesn't move. He can't hear her words. All he sees is his boy.

When we were in this backyard working on our project together ... and you forgave me. One year ago.

Alex?

His memory is fine. He seems content. He's pleasant. And most importantly, he's safe. But the true price of fixing him, manipulating something so sacred, is now clear: that boy never came back.

And all Kevin could do was watch this beautiful, acceptable creation climb the steps and enter their home.

32. Curtain Call

Brake lights and road flares. Everything red tinged. Everything constricting around Kevin, and inside him.

They crawl through the bottleneck past pounding jackhammers. Grace sighs and taps her foot.

"I know this isn't a good time," she wills the words out of her mouth, "but yesterday at the hospital, that woman in red? She came from upstairs."

"What?"

"I thought no one knew but the people from the team."

Kevin nods.

"She was up there, and so was Lawrence Kedge. He walked right past me."

"Kedge? Wasn't he—"

"The senator."

Kevin grips the steering wheel tighter.

"Father of James's piece of shit commanding officer that fired him."

"And grandfather to James's piece of shit student," she says with alarm.

Dad, what did you do? You rage at me for telling Grace, then you bring strangers into this? What did you give up? He remembers the click of James's lighter. *See the flame. Steady, burn it all, then begin again.*

By the time they arrive at *The Nightcap*, Kevin's world has gone dark. And so have *The Nightcap*'s windows.

Kevin turns off the ignition. He looks past Grace, searching for movement behind the blinds.

"Wouldn't James hire a bartender to cover when he's out?" she asks.

He peers into the dark alley and feels a chill along his scalp from when he was left there, bleeding. "Back room."

They make their way along the oil-stained asphalt to the door. It's locked.

"Nothing about this is right," Kevin says.

She nods slowly and kisses his worried cheek before dropping to a knee. She pulls out her key knife and plunges it into the lock.

Click, click, click ... click ... click. The door creaks open. Pitch black.

Kevin turns on his phone's flashlight and enters. Nothing out of the ordinary.

She follows close behind. There's a gleam on her knife edge.

He shuts the door and feels it give. He inspects the doorframe.

"Was that always there?" she whispers.

Kevin runs his hand over a vertical split in the wood. "I don't know." His voice is tight.

They collect themselves at the curtain. Hands trembling, he parts it; ghosts scatter, avoiding the beam cutting through the void. Pool table, bar, memorial to Judy. Everything where it should be.

"If he's not home and not here, where is ..." She stops. His office door is wide open. Along the frame, another split. Inside, only darkness.

Kevin slides her behind him and creeps into the bar. He grabs a bottle, heart pounding in his throat. Armed, he peeks into the room. "James?"

He flashes to the four walls and turns on the light. Same as it's always looked. A spartan desk to his right flanked by a filing cabinet on one side and bookshelves in the corners. "Maybe he lost his phone."

He examines the nineteen-eighties linoleum, and his jaw locks. Black scuff marks lead to the desk and near the closest leg, a small splatter. *Blood.*

"Oh, Kevin. No, no, no."

His eyes sweep the desk. Magazines stacked on the side, his accounting pad squarely in the middle with two parallel pens on the right. *James isn't this neat.*

Closer.

The corner of the accounting paper is torn off.

Kevin smells old leather. He's drawn to the bookshelf next to him. James's baseball glove.

His vision narrows. Shallow, automated breaths.

Closer.

He sees the familiar "J.D." tattooed in faded marker on the Rawlings pad. He picks it up. Underneath, the piece of torn paper.

"Grace." He mouths, but no words escape. His heart exits the elevator at his neck. He brings the scrap under the light. Then everything stops.

Scribbled across the front:

And on the back:

Test Subject 3
Interaction 1

I hear a moan. It's close.

It sounds like my voice.

Why can't I see anything?

Something shifts. I feel the weight of my arms, my legs, but I can't move.

A small white circle appears. Size of a dime.

Am I in a tunnel?

Now it's the size of a quarter. I'm moving towards it.

Smoke floats in from the edge. It forms a face to my right, but it's incomplete. It's missing a jaw.

Brody. No! He dissolves back into smoke and rushes into my mouth, my nose. *What are you doing?!* I choke.

The circle vibrates, building strength.

Boom.

It floods my vision. My eyes ache as I'm wrenched into bright, harsh surroundings. Mumbling. Swirling. Nauseous. *Stop!* I try to slow my breathing. My hand instinctively searches for my lighter.

I still can't move.

Blurry shapes.

Ride it out. Almost there!

Colors. Details.

High definition.

I'm in a small room on a metal chair, metal table. One man across from me. Two-way mirror over his shoulder.

"How was your trip?" he asks softly.

I struggle to move my lips; my tongue is clumsy. *Shit, I'm drooling.* I shift in my seat but can only slide my feet. I'm zip tied to the chair.

He snatched me up. No, there were more. They broke into *The Nightcap.*

"You put up quite a fight in the van. We tried benzos to sedate you but that did nothing, so went with the tried-and-true ketamine."

Zip ties, sedation meds. *These fuckers are military.*

I size up my target. American, or he has a great dialect coach. Well groomed, buzz cut, light eyes, neck tattoo of a scorpion, calm. I have about thirty pounds on him.

He notices. "I'm sure you'd kill me in a second. But I wouldn't advise that. Let's just say we have other options to address your skill set." He grabs a manila folder and opens it. "Can you state your name, please?"

I search the room for clues. Ketamine. Van. I couldn't have gone far. At most one state over. The door is cracked behind me. There's a small breeze coming through. I can hear muffled traffic in the distance. Urban.

He sighs. "How about I start? You're James Dowd, from Long Grove, Illinois. Father, deceased. Mother currently resides at Sunnyville nursing home. No siblings."

I stop. My eyes pierce into him.

"Graduated top of your class at BUD/S after setting two records for strength and endurance that still stand. Skilled at interrogation. SEAL team 8. Two deployments. Then started acting erratically. Bad conduct discharge."

"I see you've read my Wikipedia page," I say.

"Wasn't it a surprise when you magically popped up with Alex Bishop in Chicago? You deliver the very person we were looking for! And my superiors already had such fond memories of you."

I glance at the mirror. *What?*

"You won't find help there. The Bishops send their regards, but they're long gone. They left you all alone, James."

What. The. Shit.

Kevin ... Greg ... they wouldn't do this to me. They couldn't have.

"What was the last thing you said to your commanding officer? I think it was 'I'm coming for you?'" He slides up his sleeve. Two black crossed cannons. *Navy.*

No. Kedge. He's here.

"You're defiant and hostile, but frankly, that's why you're the star of the show now. I look forward to really getting to know you, just like I did with Alex. We're hoping for a similar, well-adjusted outcome. The only difference is we plan to keep you around."

"Never. I'll find a way out of here, dead, or alive."

"When this is done, your compliance will be refreshing." He sits upright. "But we're getting ahead of ourselves. Let's see your full range, and don't hold back, okay? Or, we'll kill your mother. Slowly."

"What the fuck did you just say?!"

"That's better." He smiles. "Let's begin."

Thanks for reading.

Enjoy the book? Please consider leaving an honest review on Amazon.

Interested in exclusive content like character profiles and my real stories from the ER, along with exciting updates? Visit www.tcsolomon.com where you can sign up for the newsletter.

ACKNOWLEDGMENTS

I am forever grateful to my family, friends, and new colleagues. They were instrumental in the creation of this book.

I would like to apologize to, and thank my wife, Sophie, who has been incredibly patient and supportive of my writing process. Thank you for your sincere, deep love, and thank you for keeping our home afloat and our fur baby alive while I was locked away in the office.

My mother, Annie, and my father, George, were with me since day one of both my life, and this book. I love you, and I am so appreciative of our brainstorming sessions, rounds of editing, and chapter walk-throughs in your living room. Your kindness and selflessness are unmatched.

A special thanks to my friends who have helped me every step of this journey. Alana, Anastasia, Carrie, Eric Cl., Eric Cu., John, Kirsten, Laura E., Laura F., Maddie, Mike, Noelle, Patricia, Peter, and Rosa, I am in your debt.

This has also been an international effort, and I have met fantastic new colleagues across the globe. Laura Joyce, your developmental editing, proofreading, and copy editing were the perfect fit. Thank you for helping me bring my vision to life. Dragan Bilic, and the designers at MiblArt, your cover designs were phenomenal. I hope we can continue to work together going forward. Denis Caron, my marketing guru, thank you for going above and beyond in our sessions together. Your insight was invaluable.

And last, but not least, thank *you*, again, for reading this book. Connecting with you is why I started this path in the first place.